Memories

Of...

by

CAROL M
MOTTERSHEAD

A catalogue record of the author's books is available at the British Library

ISBN: 9798 3873 1086 7

This book is a work of fiction.

The historical events are genuine, but the incidents portrayed regarding the lives of the characters are purely the work of the author's imagination.

I dedicate this book to my family with
All my love, now and forever

The author of this poem is unknown, but I'm sure they would be happy to know that their words are being shared, so, whoever you are, wherever you may be, this is a tribute to you – Thank you!

Our family is like the branches of an old but sturdy tree.

The leaves resemble people that make up our ancestry.

The past has not been easy, and it could have made it fall,

But the roots are cemented firmly, for this tree to stand so tall.

As time goes by its certain that the leaves will wither and wilt,

But the branches will thrive, on foundations they have built.

Together we are stronger, it isn't hard to see

that every leaf is needed to make this family tree.

A friends is one that know you as you are,

Understands where you have been,

Accepts what you have become,

And still, gently allows you to grow.

William Shakespeare

Preface

John first appears as a character in my book, 'Joan', where he grew up with his adopted family. Joan, his mother, Pulcinella, his father and their son Nicholas his step-brother were all part of a troupe of actors known as 'Commedia dell arte', in the seventeenth century.

John had always dreamed of excitement and adventure in foreign lands, so when he sees an opportunity to travel the high seas to a new world, he signs up to seven years as an indentured servant with Hugh Gwynn on his tobacco plantation in Virginia. The voyage is long and arduous, but it's a journey of a lifetime; an opportunity that John has been seeking all his life!

When I first created John in my earlier book, he was a fictional character. But then later, I discovered that there was actually a real person known as John Punch who lived in Virginia during the same time period, I just had to check it out.

There are only two historical records to prove that John Punch even existed; 4th June and 9th July 1640. Armed with only these two documents, the story you are about to read, was created –

We join John on Gwynn's Island, Virginia, USA in 1654. An unidentified disease has broken out all over the island. Water has become contaminated.

People are dying. John's wife Ann, is seriously ill. Things look bleak for her. John has heard that there is a medicine woman with the ability to cure all illnesses somewere to the north. The journey will be hazardous, with dangerous creatures, rugged wilderness and tidal waterways to cross. It is said that she is visiting natives. Indians who just a few months earlier had been at war with the colonists. There is peace at the moment, between them, but for how long is unknown.

The document on the next page is believed to be the true record of events, but read on for there may be more than first meets the eye. As fictitious as my story is, some names remain true, whilst others have been changed or made up when none is known. Call it literary licence if you will.

Edited by
H. R. McILWAINE

RICHMOND, *Virginia*
MCMXXIV

June 4, 1640.

Upon the petition of *Hugh Gwyn* gen' wherein he complained to this board of three of his fervants that are run away to *Maryland* to his much lofs and ҏjudice and wherein he hath humbly requefted the board that he may have liberty to make [10] the fale or benifit of the faid fervants in the faid *Maryland* which the Court taking into Confideration and weighing the dangerous confequences of fuch ҏnicious ҏcident *do order* that a letter be written unto the faid Governour to the intent the faid fervants may be returned hither to receive fuch exemplary and condign punifhment as the nature of their offence fhall juftly deferve and then be to be returned to their faid mafter ·

June 30, 1640.

The court hath granted that a commiffion fhall be drawn for *John Mattrom* and *Edward ffleet* authorizing them to levy a party ¹⁴ of men, or more if need require, out of the trained band for *Charles river* county with arms and ammunition to go in ҏfuit of certain runaway negroes and to bring them in to the governor. *And it is further ordered* that fuch men as fhall be preffed for this expedition fhall receive their pay and fatisfaction for their pains at the public charge of the counties from whence fuch negroes are runaway and likewife for any boat or boats that fhall be taken for the faid fervice.¹⁵

9ᵗʰ of *July*, 1640.

Whereas Hugh Gwyn hath by order from this Board Brought back from *Maryland* three fervants formerly run away from the faid *Gwyn*, *the court doth therefore order* that the faid three fervants fhall receive the punifhment of whipping and to have thirty ftripes apiece one called *Victor*, a *dutchman*, the other a *Scotchman* called *James Gregory*, fhall firft ferve out their times with their mafter according to their Indentures, and one whole year apiece after the time of their fervice is Expired. By their faid Indentures in recompenfe of his Lofs fuftained by their abfence and after that fervice to their faid mafter is Expired to ferve the colony for three whole years apiece, and that the third being a negro named *John Punch* fhall ferve his faid mafter or his affigns for the time of his natural Life here or elfewhere.¹⁶

CAROL M
MOTTERSHEAD

Chapter One

'Ann, did I ever tell you about the first time I saw you?' John smiled as he held his wife's hand, giving it a momentary squeeze. 'You were lying on the ground. You'd been hanging out the washing. What a sight you were, all red and burnt from the noon-day sun. I scooped you up... you were as light as a feather, so frail, your body so limp. You needed shade and quick.' John paused, checking to see if she could hear him. 'Master Hugh's house was nearest; I carried you inside, into the kitchen, and placed you on the large table in the centre of the room – it was large enough for you back then, anyway,' he teased, 'No one was at home. Everyone had gone into town. Everyone on the plantation who could be spared from working in the fields that is. Market day, the ships would be in, that meant fresh supplies from England and other lands. It was hours before anyone was due back.

I'd been left behind to make room for fresh supplies. Anything deemed inedible was to be set aside for the animals or slung into a stew pot if cook got hold of them first' laughed John, seemingly talking to himself. 'It wasn't my usual job, which was lucky for you, or I wouldn't have found you. It was pure chance that I was passing – you could have died right there and then if I hadn't. It must have been your lucky day' he laughed at a fleeting thought, 'cos look what you ended up with... me!' he chuckled, hoping to get a reaction. 'If I hadn't found you...' he watched her face as he spoke, 'it doesn't bear thinking about.' His face changed to being serious, 'I think that's when I fell in love with you,' not one to stay serious for long, he smiled at the memory. Then once again his face became anxious when he saw no reaction. Talking now, more for his own benefit, he continued: 'You were so helpless. I got you inside as quickly as I could. The kitchen was lovely and cool, a welcome change from the blazing heat of the sun...' mid sentence, John paused, noticing Ann's breathing had changed, she had fallen asleep, the hint of a smile appeared to have formed around her lips, *at least that's what he chose to believe, she looked so frail...*

Placing her hand beside her on the bed, he sat back in his seat exhausted. Usually Ann was robust and healthy, as strong as any man; she could be quite formidable when she was roused! Whatever was ailing her had to be pretty bad, even Hugh his friend and master was concerned, so much so, that he had sent for the doctor. John told himself it was not yet time to worry; Ann would pull through. *Besides,* he told himself, *the only time you to worry, is when they call the priest!* He tried to shake away his own concerns, not wanting to show any anxiety, not in front of Ann at least. John was always the strong one. The one, others relied on but now... he had never felt so helpless – so alone. Ann was the only woman is his life - other than his mother... and Mary-Anne of course.

Mary-Anne

John sat silent, his eyes closed, lost in his own thoughts... He had met Mary-Anne that day in the kitchen, the day he'd taken Ann into the house. After seeing to Ann's burns, they had sat talking while Ann was resting on the table. Mary-Anne told him how she and her husband Septimus had set off for the colonies together. Septimus was going to be valet to the master and she was to work in the kitchens as kitchen maid. Unfortunately, her husband died en route to the new world. Mary-Anne had worked her way up through the ranks eventually becoming housekeeper in charge of the whole household. Even when she had worked off her indentures she stayed with Master Hugh and his family. Being a widow, Mary-Anne had gone past wanting to own her own piece of land and all it entitled her to. She had been with the master for seven years; she'd become close to the family, the children. All in all, she had quite a comfortable life and she was content where she was. She passed away a few years later. Some say it was with a broken heart.

Ann wakens

Ann was beginning to rouse, licking her lips. Hugh had sat with John in silence, listening to him as he spoke gently to his wife. He hoped, in the silence, that John might himself had taken a few moments to nod off, but as soon as he called for Alice, the housemaid who had been hovering nearby, to fetch fresh water, John became alert, opening his eyes to check immediately on Ann. Alice poured fresh water that she'd boiled earlier in the day and left to cool. She poured a glass and handed to Hugh as a matter of urgency; he handed it to John.

Raising Ann's head with one hand, John put the glass to her lips, but in his typical clumsy way, he lifted the glass too high and almost choked her! Ann began coughing and spluttering, but despite almost being drowned by her husband, she could only laugh at the situation. She looked at her husband, her eyes speaking volumes for her, and John knew exactly what she meant – typical John, full of good intentions.

Alice ran to help dry her off, but John took the cloth from her; Ann was his wife, she was his responsibility and he was letting her down. He settled her back on the pillow. Even being moved as gently as he could, tired her out. He felt useless! Despite John's clumsiness, his wife lay with a smile on her face. *What must she be thinking?* He wondered. She tried again to sip some water. Alice, this time, offered the water to her lips and Ann managed a sip one or two before coughing again. Every effort was a strain. She needed rest. *Sleep would be good for her,* he told himself, but it left him sitting with his thoughts, in silence. Even the presence of his friend Hugh, although much appreciated, was of little consolation. Hugh could see John needed himself, to rest. Touching John on the shoulder, he nodded to John and indicated he was leaving but would be back, he left John alone with his wife hoping that in his absence, John would try to rest. He hadn't left Ann's side since she became ill, not even to eat; a short rest would do him good. Besides, there was work to be done; preparations to be made... in case the worst should happen. He hated thinking that way, but he had to do something... and practical-matters were all he could think of doing right now!

Thoughts wander back to Mary-Anne

John allowed his thoughts to wander once more to Mary-Anne. *Mary-Anne would have known what to do* he thought. She was a fountain of knowledge on such things. He missed her no nonsense pragmatism and forthrightness.

He remembered the first time he met her. She was just returning from market as John was preparing a poultice for Ann in the kitchen as she lay on the table. Ann, her pretty young face, her arms, legs and everywhere that had not been covered, were burned bright red from the scorching sun, how long she'd lain there was anyone's guess. With no one around to call on for help, John had simply gone into automatic mode. First he'd used a cloth soaked in cool water, but that wasn't enough. Then he found some potatoes, slicing them and placing them onto the burned skin kept the skin cooler for longer, which wasn't going to be enough, soon she would be awake and in pain. He had to think, think, think! Racking his brains for inspiration he remembered an old remedy of his mothers; *oatmeal, honey and milk, it would make a poultice,* that's when Mary –Anne walked in...

A short, plump, middle-aged woman demanding to know what he was doing in her kitchen! Mary-Anne, carrying a variety of parcels, suddenly noticed Ann unconscious on the table-

'What have you done to her?' she demanded. 'Help... help!' Dropping her packages, she grabbed at his arms trying to pull and push him outside. She noticed then, the mortar and pestle in his hands, he'd been grinding the oatmeal. 'What are you doing with that?' she enquired curiously. Once he'd explained his mother's recipe, he looked around the room

'I need milk or better still... honey?' looking hopeful at the angry woman standing glaring at the scene before her. Ann started to groan with pain.

'Here, give that to me. Run to the wagon outside, there's fresh honey in a jar at the rear of the wagon, and fresh milk in one of the churns, take that jug and bowl and get what we need for the poultice' ordered Mary-Anne, suddenly taking control of the stranger. A six foot black man with a young white woman lying on the table had been a bit of a shock to her, *but he seemed to have a trusting face.*

John didn't have to be told twice. He grabbed a bowl and jug from the dresser and ran to where the wagons were being unloaded. Mary-Anne was still grinding the oats when John returned. She knew exactly what to do and took charge; taking some honey and a little of the milk, she began to mix the ingredients. 'Grab those clean-cloths from off the dresser.' Ann's moans grew more frequent as she began moving restlessly on the table. Her eyes opened - a look of confusion on her face, then pain... then a scream as she saw John rushing towards her trying to stop her falling off the table. *The sight of him must have been frightening for a young lass;* he laughed to himself, *especially this ugly mug of mine* he thought. *Ann must have been so scared at their first meeting* he mused!

'Be still, you'll be fine,' said Mary-Anne in a gentle but commanding tone. 'Shush child - be still. You'll hurt yourself!' They both spoke in unison as Mary-Anne rushed to the opposite side of the table to John. Mary-Anne managed to calm Ann, explaining to her what had happened, where she was, while John stood just close enough to prevent any falls, desperate not to frighten her further. Mary-Anne continued stirring the mixture as she talked. Pointing to the corner of the room she motioned that he should fetch some rags to use. She proceeded to make poultices. Speaking calming tones to Ann she explained what they were doing, removing old cloths and replacing them with poultices. She indicated for John to help remove the old now warm cloths and she quickly replaced them directly onto Ann's skin.

Working together, it wasn't long before Ann was covered on all the necessary areas. For a little while Ann was comfortable and pain free, but that didn't last long.

'Make sure there's water in that kettle over there and put the kettle over the fire' Mary-Anne instructed John, 'Once it's come to the boil pour some into another clean jug' she added.

'Mother always said that a cup of tea made everything better.' John said, pouring water into the teapot.

'Not there boy!' yelled Mary-Anne 'It's not for a pot of tea it's to make an infusion! Fetch that box from the dresser over there' she announced slightly irritated and pointing to the opposite side of the room. Curiosity getting the better of him, he did as he told. Mary-Anne, opening the box, took out a piece of bark.

'Willow bark" she showed John the item then placed some into a fresh pot. 'Bring that kettle back to the boil and pour it boiling hot onto the bark.'

'Then what?' asked John
'Then we wait. The willow bark will infuse the boiled water and make a tisane, a potion to ease her pain. It's an old Indian recipe, they swear by it. Now pop some more water into that kettle and we'll have that pot of tea you mentioned while we wait' Mary-Anne smiled; John made them all a cup of tea *just like mother used to make* and they chattered together like old friends. Mary-Anne and John hit it off right from the start. That's when she'd told him about her Septimus; he had been a few years older than

herself, their marriage had been arranged by parents. They'd only met a few weeks before they married, but although strangers in the beginning, they soon discovered they were a good match. They had so much in common, and love came quickly to them, growing ever more each day. A few years passed and when they'd not been blessed with children of their own. Septimus decided it was time they started a new life together - in the new world. He'd heard about Colonel Hugh, his wife and son. They were looking for servants for their plantation. After much discussion, their minds were made up, they signed up and looked forward to an adventure of a lifetime! It all sounded like a fairytale romance to John, but for a moment a look of sadness crossed Mary-Anne's face.

'Not having children was a blessing in disguise' she told her new friend 'Yes – a blessing in disguise, for sure. For it gave us more time to love one another, you never know what's round the corner 'til it's too late,' and as fleeting as the momentary sadness came, it went... replaced by what John discovered to be her beautiful, reassuring, loving smile. She had been right, for their time together was cut short. Septimus caught pneumonia en route to the colonies.

Mary-Anne was not one for being maudlin and was soon giving orders once again...

'Well come on now John, we can't be sitting here chatting like old friends all this long day, you take Ann to her hut now, I'll just give you some of this tisane, Ann, then I have a meal to make for the Master.' Mary-Anne put some of the tisane into a bottle, handed it to Ann with instructions to take just a few sips whenever she felt the pain and especially before it got too bad. 'A couple of days and you should be feeling much better my dear' she said, but those dressings... they'll need changing every day 'til you're healed. You'd best be coming back after breakfast and I'll see to them for you OK? I'll inform the Mistress that you need to rest a while and I'm sure she'll be down to see you soon.' When Mary-Anne gave an order, you didn't question it. They each said their goodbyes and John carefully lifted Ann from her seat and took her home.

Ann's head lay on his shoulder as the effect of the tisane made her sleepy. They reached the hut in no time, much to John's chagrin for he didn't want their meeting to end. He felt her warm body next to his, so light was she that he could have carried her off into the sunset and never tired. It felt good to be needed and he knew right there and then *this is the girl I want to marry* and smiled.

Chapter Two

Hugh

Hugh knew he should be making his way home to Elizabeth, she'd be as worried as he himself, but he needed to clear his head. Seeing his friend attempting to stay positive and optimistic for his guest's sake was heartbreaking. *Typical of John though... not showing his true emotions* he thought. He felt an intruder. They needed to have some privacy, to have some alone time, just in case the worst happens...

Hugh, as Colonel of armies of men, had seen so much death in his time and Ann, he felt for sure, was nearing her end. He'd learned to harden his heart for the men under his command, but John... Ann... they were friends; it pained him greatly to see their suffering. Hugh knew he would have to be strong for John when the time came. He'd be the strong one when Hugh's first wife died a few years after having their youngest son. His birth had left her with a weak heart and she never fully recovered, taken in her prime. It had been Ann and John who'd helped him deal with practical things allowing him to grieve. There was nothing he wouldn't do for them, either of them. His mind momentarily unfocused as sadness washed over him.

Hugh was suddenly pulled from his reverie as he heard his name being called it was Elizabeth she must have been calling for some time before Hugh heard her for she had sent one of the male servants to grab his attention. Hugh pulled himself together sharply when the servant arrived he was given the order

'Go fetch Reverend John. Tell him his father needs him urgently. Tell him Ann... John needs him – go NOW!' and he waved his arm to signal the urgency. Hugh wandered back to the house there would be more work to do soon enough, an undertaker... Hugh paused his thoughts, there would be time enough later if the worst came to the worst, but for now Hugh refused to think of such things... not yet. His wife greeted him with concern. She knew how close he and John had become and she wanted to comfort him. He needed nourishment, he'd not slept or eaten much and was looking peaky himself, she was worried.

Elizabeth

Disease had hit the all the farms on the island. Everyone everywhere was struggling, but for Elizabeth, her main concern was for her husband. Settling Hugh down with a tankard of beer she left him to his thoughts, she hoped he'd eat something before rushing back to his friends, but she also knew she couldn't make him do anything if he didn't want to. He'd become a stubborn man since first they'd met, before his wife and family came to Virginia. He'd been young and full of enthusiasm. He was excited and full of promise and adventure that he was going to have the biggest and best plantation in Virginia. As time went on he had taken on more and more responsibilities, first the plantation then his legal work and his time commanding an army... he'd toughened up, he'd become hard. Firm but fair everyone said... firm but fair.

His eldest son was twenty-three when his mother died and his youngest was just seven years of age. With all his responsibilities and a heavy workload, Hugh had needed a nanny for the young one. Elizabeth had recently found herself in need of a job after her aunt died and had been heard that a gentleman from one of the plantations was hiring. She and Hugh met up for their second time at the interview.

It was all a bit or a whirlwind. After realising they still loved one Hugh hadn't wanted to sully her name by not marrying her and he didn't want to take the chance of losing her again. They married in front of a local magistrate and Hugh took her back to his home as his wife. *It had to have been fate giving them a second chance of happiness,* she'd thought at the time, *for what were the odds of them finding each other again and for them both to be free to marry?* She'd loved him for such a long time there had never been anyone else for her, not even when her father tried forcing her to marry. It wasn't until they were back at the plantation that Elizabeth saw Hugh was not the man she had fallen in love with – he had changed. He had built walls around his heart. He was more easily angered, less tolerant than she had remembered. His zest for life... had become jaded and the passion that she remembered so vividly... was gone! She had one thing to be thankful for, and that was the friendship with John. Hugh relied so much on him. John and his wife had extended their friendship to herself when she arrived back as Mrs Hugh Gwynn. They had become their closest friends, a friendship that was most definitely needed. Richard, the youngest boy wasn't a problem, but his eldest... was resentful of their marriage. His mother had just died a few short months earlier, Elizabeth understood, but she loved Hugh.

Chapter Three

A first kiss

Ann roused. Her eyes opened. Turning her head towards John she could see he was sleeping... dreaming... and she hoped his dreams were good ones.

Mustering all the strength she had, she reached out to him; slowly, gently, painfully, her hand, reaching out as far as she could; she stroked his cheek. His eyes opened at her touch and he smiled sleepily. As he turned to face his wife, taking her hand in his, he noticed the momentary wince on her pale face as she struggled to balance. Laying her back onto her pillow, she closed her eyes once more. He loved his wife so much. His heart longed to see her healthy and happy once again, but his fears for her life were overwhelming. Leaning in, he kissed her softly, her lips were still warm and tender... like the first time they'd kissed...

He remembered it as clearly as if it were yesterday... Harvesting had just ended. Tobacco leaves had been hung to dry in sheds and Master Hugh was in fine spirits. A pitcher of Flip had been made, and everyone was to fill their beakers for a special announcement. All workers were given the whole of the evening off and did not need to return to work until noon the next day! What a treat – especially when we were told that there would be no need for segregation, men, women and children could all celebrate together! Most everyone was taking advantage of the rare opportunity to revel in one another's company; feasting, drinking, laughing, dancing was just the tip of the iceberg, as people cavorted all about. John only had eyes for one person. He had seen Ann standing amongst a group of young maidens, who themselves were under the scrutiny of the older women. He approached her, looking directly at her whilst bowing his head; his beaker held high in greeting, dancing to the beat of the music; feet shuffling first to the left, feet not crossing, then shuffling to the right, feet not crossing, and repeating as he approached grinning for ear to ear in a mischievously teasing fashion. The men folk taunted John as he danced, calling him Jim Crow as his dance resembled that of a crow dancing around a bucket attempting to grab food.

Despite their teasing of him, they joined him in his dance; copying his movements in front of Ann and the ladies. As he neared, he stretched out a hand for her to join him. She laughed shyly, embarrassed by the attention. Eventually, John managed to coax Ann to dance with him after much egging on by the men, and women, around them. Handing his beaker to one of the men he and Ann danced the rest of the evening together. The music was exhilarating and exciting and soon the couple were exhausted with delight.

Daylight was fading as the evening wore on, but still warm for the time of year, autumn, it was always John's favourite time of year. All the hard work was behind them, there would be a lull before preparing the fields once again for planting.

John walked Ann towards the apple trees where they could sit and shelter in the cool breeze wafting in from the nearby river. Sitting on the cool grass laughing and breathless from dancing, they closed their eyes to savour the moment. Sounds from the celebrations could be heard the distance, the birds were calling to one another as they ended their day's flight; the sounds of silence... almost tangible... was a blessed relief to their ears. John sat contented, smiling to himself, happy to be spending time with his Ann. *His Ann' it sounded so good.*

Feeling the warmth from her body next to his own, he put his arm around her inviting her to lie down with him. She accepted willingly, allowing herself to be drawn down beside him, placing her own arms about his body, their closeness seemed natural.

They lay enjoying each other's company for some time before John opened his eyes. He lazily propped himself on his elbow to look down at Ann. A peaceful, content look radiated from her beautiful petite face. *This is how it should be,* he thought, and he leaned over to kiss her on the forehead. As fate would have it, it was at that same time that Ann turned to look up at John and instead of kissing her head their lips met... fleetingly. It was only a moment in time, but if felt to John that Ann had kissed him back, *had she been about to kiss him* he wondered?

Embarrassed, they both stood up quickly, brushing themselves down to remove any grasses. John started to knock grass off Ann's skirt, then realised the familiarity of what he was doing and felt suddenly embarrassed. *They'd only had this one evening together and already he was taking liberties… or was he?* He wasn't sure if Ann was upset or embarrassed. Stumbling with his words, he stopped trying to speak, instead, he held out an arm for her to take, *to help with her balance crossing the grasses on the way home* he told himself. Ann, looking flustered, continued to brush herself down, removing imaginary leaves and grass from her hair, tidying herself up. Once content that she looked respectable she took his proffered arm; they walked home in awkward silence.

Chapter Four

Ann-Joyce versus Elizabeth

Hugh sat on the porch staring out over the land. His dear wife Elizabeth sat close by darning socks, a task normally carried out by maids, but Elizabeth found it relaxing. She was different from his first wife Ann.

Ann-Joyce, at first, so delicate in nature, soon found living on the plantation tiresome, she'd been used to townships all her life and life as a wife on a plantation was simply boring. She ran his household well enough, firm but fair to the servants, but Hugh never seemed to make her happy. Ann-Joyce was used to the social life back in England. To her credit, she was dutiful and supported Hugh in building up his status in the community. She was proud of him when he became the local Justice of the Peace and even more proud of him when he became a member of the House of Burgesses. It meant attending social occasions and meeting local gentry which Ann-Joyce loved. She made the perfect host and a most delightful escort for any event.

When Hugh was away with the army, it was Ann-Joyce who ran the plantation in his absence, with the help of John. Becoming Colonel at such a young age meant that Ann-Joyce got plenty of practice at being in charge, being her own boss, being independent – she was in her element, until she became ill.

Elizabeth on the other hand, his beautiful and kind Elizabeth, was different. She was more loving and attentive, appreciative even. Elizabeth's life hadn't been easy. She had learned, long ago, her place in society. Her family, early immigrants to the new world, had lived through harsh times, they'd worked hard for everything they had. Meeting Hugh had been her downfall.

They met when he was on a long journey to Maryland. Elizabeth joined the waggon train along the route from King William. It was an arduously long journey, almost three days due to inclement weather. With nothing more to do but talk, they chattered and laughed together the whole of the long journey. Elizabeth appeared to be quite educated for a young woman. They found they had such a lot in common. They became close. Too close in fact.

Arriving in Maryland found them both feeling a little sad as they reluctantly parted ways. It had been some time since Hugh had spoken with such an interesting woman, or spoken in fact to any woman, interesting or not! His wife was in England with her family awaiting the birth of their first child. The day he had told her he was taking them to the new world to live, was the day she told him she was with child. It had been agreed that she would join him after the baby was born and when she felt able to travel. That was two years ago!

Elizabeth was young and of marriageable age. Her aunt had requested her presence for a short visit as she *'had a surprise'* her parents told her. That surprise turned out to be to introduce her to the man she was to marry; a man fifteen years her senior and her father had given his approval! Elizabeth was outraged! She was an educated woman, with a mind of her own! There would be no marriage to anyone unless she agreed! So upset, distraught and angry was she that she ran back into town, not knowing where she was heading and landed smack bang in Hugh's arms as she rounded a corner crying uncontrollably with sheer anger!

As it turned out, Hugh had completed his business and was staying at a local hostelry awaiting the returning waggon train to Jamestown. He took Elizabeth back to the hotel. Finding them a table, he ordered food and wine for them both and listened intently to Elizabeth's story, trying, without much luck, to calm down her rage. He knew it shouldn't have happened, Elizabeth was vulnerable; but he had taken her to his room intending to sleep in the chair. Half way through the night he had heard Elizabeth's muffled crying and sat on the bed *to comfort her that was all...* he told himself, then he kissed her. Whether it was a true kiss of affection or rebellion at having been *'given'* to a stranger like a piece of unwanted chattel Hugh never knew, but it felt good. Elizabeth was young and innocent. Slowly he began to remove her clothes; watching her face, her young beautiful face. At first he wasn't sure if he should continue, then Elizabeth began unbuttoning his shirt and he knew she was accepting of his attention.

They made love all night, first slow and tender then as passions arose, their love-making became more amorous until finally they were both spent and exhausted naked and breathless. Holding one another tightly; fear that letting go would allow reality back into their lives, allow their conscience to strike... and feelings of guilt!

They watched the dawning light as the sun rose above the rooftops, quietly enjoying the closeness of one another's naked body, content in the silence after a night of unforgettable passion. Each knew that what they had done was wrong, but the moment was theirs. A memory that was to last them for a lifetime.

Chapter Five

John

Ann had once again fallen into a slumber this time restless, her arms randomly flailing about uncontrollably, beads of perspiration on her forehead. John dripped water onto her dry lips and placed a cool cloth on her forehead. He had to do something he couldn't just sit here and watch his wife die! *He had to do something*. The words kept going round in his head, but what could he do?

Tears were now freely running down his cheeks. The doctor looked at Ann, then at John; a knowing nod of understanding passed between the two men. Ann's time was getting close, but John held tightly onto her hands as if to give her all his strength. There was so much they still wanted... no – needed, to share together. They'd had such a good life until now. *Dear Lord, please... just a little more time...* begged John silently.

Holding onto her for as long as possible, he tried talking to her once again. *If only he could make her laugh or smile again, just once more...*

'Do you remember our first dance, Ann?' John laughed nervously looking for some sign that she could still hear him. He paused to compose himself before continuing, 'You smiled shyly as I approached you. The women-folk found it amusing to see me dancing the way I did, the men calling me Jim Crow as I shuffled towards you like a crow seeking out its prey. I held out my right hand for you to take, carrying a beaker of freshly heated flip in the other. Closer and closer till you could reach my hand' John was laughing, mostly to himself, but so desperate was he to be heard by Ann.

'You just laughed at first, but while you laughed I took your hand and pulled you towards me. You stepped a little closer and almost tripped into my arms' John chuckled... it looked like his Ann smiled as if... *was she too remembering that first shared moment? John continued hopefully...*

'I caught your fall and lifted you into dancing with me and your face became flushed and excited as we danced. Everyone was copying my dance... our dance. We looked like a murder of crows. We danced 'til we dropped!' He laughed lightly once again, Ann, eyes still closed, appeared to be smiling at the memory.

'Try not to overdo it, John, you don't want to tire her out too much, she's becoming breathless. Try to rest awhile, Ann,' urged the doctor.

'How dare you John' Ann, struggling to speak, laughed weakly with a smile. John tried to keep his voice light and playful.

'Dare what?' John grinned cheekily at his wife, trying to look innocent and failing

'I'm a good girl, I am' teased Ann remembering what followed.

'You are definitely my favourite girl' joked John teasingly back at her knowing exactly what she was referring to. Fleetingly her eyes opened. They shared a tender look at one another and she tried to squeeze his hand at their shared memory; a shared 'secret' memory known only to themselves.

Ann fell into a peaceful slumber – smiling, the look of contentment, the face of an angel. Ann was John's first and only true love. Other than the love of his Mother and his friendship with Mary-Anne, there had been no other woman in John's life and he loved and treasured them all unconditionally, each in their own unique ways.

A quick word with Hugh and he knew what he had to do. He had heard that the Moyaone Indians had a stranger living among them; a medicine woman they described as *being as beautiful as the moon, wise beyond her years, and who was able to cure all illnesses...* or so the stories told.

It would be a three-day ride to where he needed to be, provided Hugh would let him use his best and fastest horse - four days at most. Kissing Ann warmly on her now cooling lips, he was fearful that this could be the last time he saw her. Should he stay or should he go? To stay meant sure death to go - he had hope. Hope that it wouldn't be too late! Tearing himself away from her side, he put food and fresh water that Alice had boiled, into a bag preparing for what would be a long journey over some hard and treacherous terrain, and ran to the stables. He had to try, he had to save her! He loved her so much. He wanted one more chance to make his wife's dream come true... her dream had always been to be married by a

Jesuit priest in her church; to be finally married in the eyes of her God. *Dear God, if I achieve nothing else in this life please, I pray with all my heart and soul, grant us this one last journey together?*

Chapter Six

Elizabeth's story

From sheer exhaustion, Hugh had fallen into a deep, but short sleep on the veranda of his home. How long he'd been asleep was anyone's guess, but as he opened his eyes he noticed Elizabeth still sitting beside him. This time, having finished darning the socks from earlier, she was now knitting away quietly. She had placed a beaker of beer next to him at some point, and a plate of bread and cheese for when he awakened. She felt him jerk awake, but didn't speak, she didn't even look at him; Elizabeth just sat in a *companionable silence* waiting for him to fully awaken. Hugh was silent too, watching her as she worked diligently on her latest task. *This woman never stops* he thought, *always on the go, never truly resting.*

Elizabeth had learned a long time ago not to nag Hugh, especially when his eyes first opened. It wasn't that she was on tenterhooks with him, for she knew his temper came purely from the frustrations of his daily life and not with her; but allowing him to adjust his thoughts, made him less niggled with her.

When she had first met Hugh, he was young, with a keen enthusiasm for his new life in this new world. The life and responsibility of a plantation owner was simpler times back then; everyone was equal, all in the same boat... masters and servants alike. Surviving the hostile elements was their only true enemy, the environment, the weather. Natives were wary of the newcomers, but friendly enough... in the beginning at least, even helping the settlers from time to time.

The occasional gossip had reached Elizabeth's ears during their years apart. She had heard how he was a respected member of the community amongst his neighbours, friends and his workforce. Even when he became Justice of the Peace in York County and a member of the House of Burgess in Charles River County, he was reputed as being firm but fair, but that was before they re-united, before they were married. Even during the early days of their marriage, after more than twenty years apart, they were happy.

Their first encounter all those years ago left more than a blot on Elizabeth's reputation it had left her with a child. She refused to marry the elderly man her father had chosen for her even when she found she was pregnant, and he would have given her child his name, stability, status, Elizabeth refused. She was stubborn. She had loved Hugh from their first night together. Her father had been furious! He'd wanted to shame Hugh into marrying her.

The day they went to the Gwynn plantation, the door was answered by a woman with a young child in her arms approximately one or two years of age. The woman was closely joined by Hugh himself. Elizabeth remembered that day as if it were yesterday. Her father stepped forward when he saw Hugh at the door, but Elizabeth grabbed her father by the arm, shook her head, and bowed her head in shame. Her father as angry as he was, stepped back for an instant, and then in one wild swing, he struck

Hugh a hard blow! Hugh fell to the floor with one fell swipe. Her father stormed off, dragging Elizabeth behind him. She'd looked back at Hugh, checking to see if he got up, worried that her father may have caused serious injury, and seeing his arms reaching for his face, the woman kneeling beside him, the young child crying, she left. Nothing more was said. Her father never spoke his name again. Her mother never spoke of him again.

Outcast from polite society, Elizabeth became known as a 'thornback', an aged spinster of the parish. The child was raised as one of her siblings. No one ever asked about the sudden appearance of a baby, nor was the matter discussed ever again; it was almost like nothing had happened. Elizabeth felt stripped of her motherhood. Her parents did allow her one concession, she was allowed to give her son a name, she named him John Gwyn; for in the bible John meant 'graced by God' which she felt was true, and Gwyn… well Gwyn meant 'beautiful, fair-haired, white, blessed and holy' and to Elizabeth, he was all of those things... For over the years, he'd been her strength when times were tough, he'd shown her unconditional love when no one else seemed to care, and he was all she had of Hugh to remember him by. To Elizabeth he was her life.

For years she accepted that everything that her family did was for the best. Her father had insisted that the child be given the family name of Fielding so as not to bastardise him unnecessarily and for that she was thankful, and to the outside world Elizabeth was a respected and loyal daughter, but out of sight she was made to feel less than a servant. Her mother tried her best to put it all behind them, but her father, who once treated her as his princess, now kept her at a distance. He never really forgave her for letting down his family name. Elizabeth had lost the love of her father, a bond that they never regained. He died leaving Elizabeth feeling a big disappointment to him.

Because Elizabeth had refused to marry, her father sent her away, to act as companion to an elderly aunt and local socialite. She was kept busy doing chores, shopping, fetching and carrying, occasionally being treated to a night out with the aunt, acting as her escort. Mindless chatter was discouraged by the old lady, but she was allowed half a day off once a month and she would spend it with her son. A special bond grew from those half-days once a month as Elizabeth showered love on her son every chance she had.

Elizabeth learned there could be strength in silence. She learned to speak only when spoken to, and to keep her head down if she wished not to be scolded. When the elderly aunt died she felt little or no sadness for the old lady other than the fact that she was soon to become homeless. News of an opening for a housekeeper-come-nanny, reached the ears of her mother.

'It is for a prominent member of the House of Burgess, a respectable gent' her mother told her. 'This could be the making of you my girl. If you get this job, it could be a position for life, you mark my words!' Arrangements were made for her to meet with the widower that weekend.

Interviews were being carried out in a back room of a local hostelry, a double-storey building with a few rooms for guests and stables at the rear. Men were sat in the bar watching entertainment on a make-shift stage where some female was singing or more precisely, shouting a song over the noise of the crowd. A bar man walked towards the end of the bar, signalling for her to join him. After asking what she wanted in not such a polite manner, he directed her to a door the stairs in the foyer, telling her to knock first and wait to be called in. Elizabeth knocked, but no one answered. She stood uncomfortably waiting for a reply and was about to leave when a young woman came out looking rather serious and not too happy.

'You can go in now' she told Elizabeth and walked off like a peacock with a sore a*** Elizabeth didn't like to finish that train of thought, but it was funny when Jack said it once in describing the old lady. She smiled to herself at the memory, and walked into the room.

The room was small, with a man standing at the open window looking out, visibly taking in a deep breath and sighing before turning round to face the next interviewee. She was totally taken aback when she saw his face. He was older than when she last saw him, it was more than twenty years that had passed - Hugh was the widower she was sent to interview for!

Twenty long years they'd been apart yet when their eyes met... it was like all those years just fell away. Hugh was a little grey around the temples, Elizabeth a little fuller of figure, but the feelings... Oh those wonderful feelings... came flooding back – it was as if it had been yesterday that they'd seen one another!

Embarrassed as they were, they were soon holding each other closely. Neither wanting to let go of the other for fear it was just a dream. Elizabeth's heart was racing. The smile on her face felt fit to crack! They clung together for what seemed an age...

Eventually, they parted... sat down to talk. Neither knew where to start. They both spoke at once and laughed... It had been a long time since Elizabeth had dared to laugh with a man. She felt young again. The love she felt had no words to express itself. She could only smile, and smile and smile...

The room Hugh had been given to use for the interviews was a private section for diners wanting to be alone so Hugh ordered food and drink for them both. It felt as natural as if no time had passed at all. Hugh told Elizabeth about his wife and their two sons and about her death and Elizabeth told him about her life, omitting to tell him about her son... their son. Jack was her pride and joy, but she wasn't sure how Hugh would react to discovering she had a child, let alone that the child was his! It wasn't that she was ashamed of him or anything, just that... *she needed the job,* she told herself. All manner of thoughts were flashing through her mind while they ate.

Her parents had moved house twice after discovering Elizabeth was with child. Once before she started showing and again after the child was born

'A new life with a new baby, no one outside of the family will ever know the truth.' Her father told her. But Elizabeth and John knew the truth, it was their secret. John had never asked about his father. How would she break the news to him after all this time anyway? Would he be angry? Would he call her names? Would he hate her? Those were all the questions running through her head as she returned home on that fateful night when she lost her son…

As the meal came to an end Elizabeth was left with one thought… how was she going to tell Hugh he had another son?

Chapter Seven

John – The journey

John had last heard that the strange and enigmatic medicine woman was living with the Powhatan Indians at the northern-most part of Potomac River. It was said that her face was as pale as the moon, and that she had magical powers that could cure any illness. There had been many sightings of her over the previous few months, always moving from village to village or disappearing with the moon for weeks at a time. John was determined to find her, and he knew that he had to reach her before she moved to another village or she could be lost to him forever.

Master Hugh had told him to take 'Greased Lightning', the fastest horse in his stables, but John knew that the old quarter-horse lacked the stamina needed for such a journey. He chose 'Major' instead – a Narraganset Pacer that would be sure-footed and sturdy on the muddy, rugged paths. Plus, he'd worked with Major before and knew that he was a good horse.

John packed supplies for the journey and checked that the horse was well shod and ready. He was a prime concern. It was mid-morning before they could get away. At this time of year, the short days and long nights meant the day's ride would be almost over before they started if he didn't leave right away. He had to see Ann before setting off; *Lord let this not be goodbye.*

Ann was still asleep. Alice was sitting with her. The doctor had left instructions to send someone to fetch him if there were any changes, but Ann's condition was deteriorating rapidly. John hovered anxiously for a moment. Should he stay or should he go? Finally, his yearning to try to save her made the final decision for him; he had to find the medicine woman, she was his only hope.

John had never journeyed so far before, but the doctor, who told him about the medicine woman, said to head north along the Rappahannock River. The Indian camp was about two or three days ride away depending on the weather and the terrain.

In the autumn months the weather could be unpredictable, but he could only hope that fate was on his side. The doctor told him that the medicine woman would be able to help his wife. She had been ill for many weeks and the doctor had done all he could. John was desperate and willing to try anything.

The sun swiftly rose to its peak as John prepared to leave; the terrain, at first, was easy to traverse, being dry and with a warm autumn breeze. A few hours had passed before daylight began to fade. Knowing they should stop to rest, John pressed onward; Major seemed to be of the same mind, as if he knew the urgency of the journey they were undertaking. Major galloped as fast as he could across the open ground, but as they came to rocky terrain, he began to stumble and slow down. He knew they had to make it to Carvers Creek before dark, so he pressed on, despite the difficult terrain.

Finally, close enough to their first stop, John gave in and decided to set up camp. He recognized some of the terrain from once before, a journey he'd made to Maryland for Master Hugh. Thirst and hunger were now getting the better of him, and he knew they both needed rest if they were to face the next leg of their journey. They would be heading over higher ground tomorrow and that they would need all the strength they could muster - e*at, drink and rest, for tomorrow would be another day.*

Working quickly, John knew he had made the right choice in selecting a strong and sturdy horse like Major. If he was to have any chance at saving Ann, he would have to take care of the horse first, before attending to himself. They were losing light; there was no time to waste.

Sleep evaded him. He had hoped that sleep would help time to pass by more quickly so he could be on his way much sooner, but his mind would have none of it. His thoughts kept flitting between concerns for the journey ahead and for his dear wife, his beautiful, beautiful wife. He was so worried about her safety, and whether or not she would be okay without him. Surely, she must be feeling just as anxious as he was. Just the thought of her being anxious and alone was enough to make him feel even worse.

He was bone-weary and mentally exhausted, he needed to sleep. He needed strength. *If his body could no longer give that to him, maybe his mind could* he thought. Maybe his mind could give him the strength to keep going. Searching his memories for something to bolster his strength and sustain him through the arduous journey, John closed his eyes and allowed his mind to wander. It didn't take long, for as always it was thoughts of his wife that always gave him his strength; she *was* his strength.

When he first met Ann she was frail and vulnerable, little did he realise the inner strength this woman possessed... not until after they were married! The thought of his five-foot-nothing, in her bare feet, wife brought a smile to his face.

Just looking at her it was hard to believe that Ann could be so formidable! She could take on anyone who stood in her way, especially when she believed she was in the right! *Just like mother,* he remembered fondly, smiling at the memory. The more he thought about it, the more he realised he'd seen a glimmer of her inner strength the day he proposed to her, *or did she propose to him*, he puzzled?

It was late spring, eight months after their first meeting. It was the day he found her lying on the ground unconscious and burned. He'd scooped her up into his arms and into the house for shelter.

Carrying her back to her hut that night John fell in love with her, it was then that he knew she would be the one for him. He wasn't so sure about how Ann felt, for Ann was shy, and she didn't give much away when it came to her feelings. What he did know though, was that he could always make her laugh. She had such a laugh, with a sort of snort at the end that was so funny it made her laughter infectious, and he laughed at the thought of her.

The next few months were tough for them, as they barely saw each other. The only time they would see each other was if they paths crossed and even then they could only wave if no one was looking. They did occasionally manage to steal a cuddle or two once in a while; every moment they could snatch was precious.

Market days were usually their best opportunities to meet up. John would often be left to prepare the storeroom for the returning supplies, while Ann was left to attend to household chores. There were the special occasions though too... when harvesting was finished, Master Hugh would give everyone the evening off to celebrate, then there was Christmas of course... John fondly remembered... He and Ann would take advantage of any time they could, they were young and in love.

If they'd been caught they would have been in for a beating, but in a way, it only added to the excitement of seeing one another. They were risking everything just to be together, and that made their love feel all the more real.

Passion between the two of them brewed until it could no longer be denied. They yearned for a closeness that could only be satiated by becoming one. The magnetic pull of each other's bodies became all-consuming, it dominated their every waking moments. Wedlock was their only solution. Ann was the first to say it! He suddenly realised, that was when she first revealed that inner strength.

As much as she longed for his body, she couldn't, or wouldn't, allow herself to be given over to her base desires.

'I'm a good girl I am, a God-fearing woman. My parents brought me up proper they did. We left England because we weren't allowed to pray to our God no more. My parents died trying to keep our faith. Father wanted us to all have a new life, a safe life, in a land where we could be free!' John wasn't sure if she was telling him or reminding herself to be *a good girl*, but he came to appreciate that her strength came from her faith and she could not bring herself to dishonour the memory of her parents. To give in to her desires to be intimate with John outside of wedlock would disgrace her family's name. 'She couldn't do it!' She had told him.

John prided himself on being a man to find solutions to problems and his first thought was to first ask permission from Master Hugh, to marry Ann in the first place. Then to ask if he would be the one to perform the marriage ceremony, for what it was worth. After all, hadn't he heard Master Hugh speak often enough about how he wanted all his workers to be part of a greater plan; to stay on or near the plantation, to build a community, and don't you need married couples and families to build a community? John was certain that the master would agree. What John hadn't anticipated, was Ann's attitude to marriage.

Ann tried to explain to John how Catholics weren't properly married unless it's in *the sight of God!* That was to cause a problem. With no church and not many Jesuit priests in Virginia, they wouldn't be able to be married in the sight of God, plus John wasn't a Christian. It was the reason he'd ran away to Maryland all those years ago. He'd heard that a priest was baptizing Indians and hoped that the master would allow him to be baptized too - then there was that mix up...

He brought his mind back to Ann. He didn't want to be thinking of the bad things that happened in his life he wanted strength from the *good* memories. He focussed on Ann once again. He remembered how the idea of getting married had set Ann on a soul-searching journey. Struggling with her faith, she had two options... either sacrifice her faith and live in sin with the man she loved and who made her happy and accept that in the eyes of God she would never be considered a wife, or take the chance of losing him. John reassured her that the final decision was hers he would stand by and honour her decision no matter what she decided. *He promised her he would be with her always to love and protect her through sickness and in health... Always and forever, he'd told her over and over again, he loved her.*

The only person Ann felt she could to turn to for understanding was Mary-Anne, the only other Catholic woman on the plantation that she knew. Ann was sure that Mary-Anne would be able to relate to how she was feeling. John was thankful for what the old lady told her.

'These are harsh times Ann,' said Mary-Anne 'Unusual and strange times. You love him don't you?' she asked, Ann nodded 'Then follow your heart my dear. Life's too short to do anything less. God will understand, he is everywhere... he'll be with you when you need him - choose love. Besides, if Master Hugh agrees to the marriage, he's the boss around here and he's the law, the Justice of the Peace isn't her!' Ann told John how Mary-Anne had given her advice then punctuated it by making a cup of tea, as if that was the end of the matter! John had to laugh, for once again he'd been reminded of his mother...

'Dear mother,' he spoke aloud to himself 'Ann is so much like you. I miss you. You'd have known what to do.' His heart reached out to his mother Joan, the first woman who had shown him any affection. 'Ann chose me, mother, she chose love! Pulling his blanket tightly around him, John drifted off to sleep holding onto that one thought – *she chose me...*

Chapter Eight

Passion rekindled

Hugh had sat quietly watching his wife as she knitted, *probably another scarf* he thought and shook his head wearily, smiling inwardly. Finishing his food and washing it down with what was left in his beaker. He made to move... his hands on the arm of his chair in which he'd been sitting. He paused... looked over at Elizabeth, *she really was so special to him* he mused. *Kind and thoughtful, forbearing of him, and did he ever show her how much he appreciated her?*

He leaned over and kissed her tenderly... gently, then, pulling her towards him he kissed her passionately... longingly. Surprised - Elizabeth didn't respond. She could only stare at him. It had been such a long time since he'd as much as shown any recognition of her in his presence, let alone kissed her! Hugh felt rejected and turned to leave, but Elizabeth grabbed his wrist and wouldn't let him go. Her knitting fell to the floor as she stood to face him. Pulling him closer to her, she tentatively returned his kiss. Hugh responded. With passion and yearning, their kisses said all they were feeling, conveying all the love and affection they both felt, but never dared to say out loud. Breathless, Elizabeth paused and looked at Hugh hopefully, longingly. Her hopes and dreams were about to be fulfilled. Hugh attempted to lift her into his arms and carry her inside, thoughtlessly trying to be young and romantic as he had once been, but he had to let her fall to her feet as realisation struck him that he was no longer a spring chicken. They laughed as her feet hit the ground with a clatter almost pulling Hugh down as she fell, but they were laughing together.

It had been a long time since they'd laughed together. Neither of them had felt able to show any feelings towards one another once they were back on the plantation. At first it was the inappropriateness they felt for Hugh being a recent widower, then as time passed, life got in the way, complacency, then acceptance that this was how life would be from now on… Love lost, even to the point of not talking to one another. But seeing John with Ann, afraid of losing her, afraid of losing one another, brought both Hugh and Elizabeth to realize that life was too short to be wasted. They'd already lost too many years of not being together. Time suddenly seemed precious. Neither wanted to waste one more second, one more minute… one more day! They made love with a passion that they had not experienced for a long time. Exhausted and breathless they lay holding one another close, neither one wanting to be the first to draw away. There was a knock on the door…

'Come quickly – it's Ann!' a voice called out.

'He's coming.' Called Elizabeth as Hugh grabbed his clothes and ran towards the door. Elizabeth followed close behind, worried… but a hint of a smile wouldn't leave her face. As guilty as she felt, she couldn't help feeling just a little happy. She and Hugh were sated with passion.

Pushing through the door of Ann's home, Hugh and Elizabeth's nostrils were hit hard with a pungent smell of garlic. Ann had been struggling for breath. The doctor had been called and created a preparation of crushed garlic added to boiling water to make a vapour which seemed to be easing Ann's breathing.

'It's time.' Hugh told Elizabeth sadly.

'Time to send for Reverend John?' Elizabeth asked, hoping it was not true – not yet! Hugh nodded. Elizabeth left the room. How could this be happening? At a time when she and Hugh were at their happiest, their friend was nearing her life's end? With a heavy heart she arranged for one of the servants to fetch her stepson.

Calling for Reverend John was the last thing either of them wanted to do, but they knew how important Ann's faith was to her. They had to be practical she would want to be given the last rights it was the least they could give her. Not knowing if their son would be near or far was always going to be problem. Often working with a parishioner could take him miles away, but they had to try... they had to be ready – for Ann's sake!

Chapter Nine

The Medicine Woman

John was very close to the Indian camp at Potomac. As he was about to enter the camp, he got down from his horse and walked slowly and carefully. He held his head high so that the Indians would not see that he was afraid. In recent years, there had been no fighting between the Indians and the colonists. But there was still a lot of distrust between them. Some tribes were more distrustful than others. John needed the Indians to trust him if he was going to ask for their help.

Although the natives were going about their business quietly, there was a natural mistrust of strangers. Outwardly, no one acknowledged his presence, but eyes watched his every movement. The sensation was almost tangible.

John walked deeper into the camp, and some children who were playing nearby saw him. One young girl ran up close to him, then stopped and stared at him when he smiled. She was scared, and turned to run, but bumped into an elderly squaw and quickly hid behind her, fearfully, shyly watching John.

John suddenly realized how he must have appeared to such a small child... tall as he was - more than eighteen hands high. And John, being of South African descent, was black as black could be; working out in the sunshine had darkened his skin even further. Even he could see why she was scared of him!

John's smile was always a bit frightening, especially with his mouthful of white teeth. His wife Ann used to tease him about it all the time.

'You're like the giant crocodile in your stories,' she would say, gnashing her teeth in a snapping, biting action as she smiled. John smiled quietly at the memory of Ann. His attention was abruptly brought back to the present by the old woman.

'Washtay,' [Hello] greeted the old squaw in her native tongue. John new enough Algonquin to reply:

'Washtay,' replied John, the old woman smiled at his efforts. Most native Indians spoke English well enough to trade with colonists and John was hoping to find someone he could communicate with.

'Washtay' he repeated when the woman stood staring. Miming as best he could he asked slowly...

'I need to speak with the medicine woman with the pale face, is she here? I need to speak to her urgently!' He hoped desperately that the woman understood. She looked John up and down as if wondering if he could be trusted. He must have won her approval because she nodded repeatedly, and turned around indicating that he should follow her.

John stroked his horse's muzzle more to keep himself calm than the horse. He followed the woman. She guided him through the camp to a lodge built on slightly higher ground. The old squaw raised her hand, indicating to John that he should stop. The child was pushed gently to one side where her mother was now waiting to take her, and a young brave took hold of the horse's reins, unsmiling, but with a nod of his head, and a gently tug on the reins with his hand, he indicated that John should let go of his horse and wait. John held onto his horse briefly, warily, watching the young brave as he made a sign for food and water for the horse... Finally understanding that the young brave simply wanted to tend to the horse, John relinquished hold of the reins and stood nervously alone. Standing outside a stranger's home, he felt vulnerable. There were no quick means of escape. Maintaining his control, he waited, outwardly patient, inwardly afraid.

Peace between the Indians and the colonists was still tentative. John reminded himself that this journey was for his wife; he had to save her or die trying! He needed to be strong. He had to see his task through to the end. His Ann meant everything to him, she needed him. She needed the healing potion. He prayed silently that the medicine woman he'd heard so much about would be here. The potion was said to heal all types of illnesses, all ills. He stood firm. He stood proud. He waited... for the medicine woman who he hoped would save his wife's life.

John waited what felt like forever, until finally a door was thrust open. There stood the imposing figure of the weroance. He was an older man, but if it weren't for the clothing he wore, he would have appeared feeble. He was wearing full Indian King head-dress distinguished with a badge made out of jewels, and a long heavy cloak ornamented with shells, surrounded by strong, young braves he made for a fearful and formidable site.

'Washtay' John said; a hand touched his arm to silence him.

The old man turned and re-entered the lodge, followed by his sons. John was guided into the lodge by braves in front and behind him. A senior looking brave indicated to John that he should sit. Others sat down too, forming a circle within the lodge. All were silent except for one who seemed to be filling a long pipe with tobacco and speaking words of some kind. John respectfully listened and waited. When the warrior paused speaking his words, John opened his mouth to speak but was once again silenced by the hand from earlier. The pipe, now lit, was handed to the Chief who breathed in the burning fumes appearing to inhale as if savouring the flavour, and passed the pipe to John. John just looked - puzzled. Holding it with both hands the Chief offered it repeatedly until John took the pipe from him. John had smoked tobacco on the plantation by way of testing the quality of the leaves but had never liked the taste. Reluctantly he took hold of the pipe and looked round the circle of Indians. All eyes were watching him including the weroance. John put the pipe to his mouth he could feel the heat already rising in its stem; the fragrance... slightly different to any he had smelled on the plantation. John wasn't quite sure what to expect. He inhaled the substance... trying to hold it in his mouth as the Chief had done, John didn't succeed and ended up coughing loudly as the smoke left his body in a sudden mass of smoke! The whole room became filled with laughter from the warriors, with only the slightest grin from the Chief as he moved his hands in a silencing motion to everyone. The pipe continued to be handed round the room in silence until the last man, and woman, had taken part in what seemed to be some sort of ritual. John remained silent.

The pipe was ceremonially laid down and the females began moving. This time food was brought in woven baskets with pouches of some sort of liquid. It was time to eat. The Chief was given food before anyone else then John was shown the serving dish. The food looked most appetizing and John had to admit to being ravenous as he'd not eaten since sunrise. Water was what he most craved more than anything; his eyes must have spoken as they lit up at the sight of the jugs of water being brought in. The Chief directed the first sip to his guest before drinking it himself. John had heard of the generosity of certain Indian tribes but was still pleasantly surprised as to how he was being treated.

Once food and drink had been shared amongst those present the Chief directed his full attention to John by introducing himself:

'Washtay. My name... Nectowane. I am Chief of Pamunkey tribe. Welcome. How may I help you?' asked the weroance in broken, but clear English. John was relieved to hear the Chief speaking in English he was wondering how he would mime certain words. It made his request easier to make knowing his host spoke his language.

'Washtay.' John attempted to respectfully greet Chief Nectowane in his own language.

'I come to you on a mission of great urgency. My wife... my dear wife, Ann, is seriously ill. I have heard you have a white woman staying with you, a medicine woman... I have great need of her assistance.' John spoke with some urgency. The chief looked at John as if scrutinising his very being. John looked pleadingly at his host. Signalling one of the braves to him, Chief Nectowane spoke something in his ear and sent him away.

'The white medicine woman you speak of is indeed still here, but she is preparing for a vision quest. It is most important that she is not interrupted unnecessarily,' said the chief.

'I fear for the life of my wife. I NEED her help... her medicine,' pleaded John.

The brave returned, followed closely by the white woman, as radiant and beautiful as he'd been told, wearing the clothing of a squaw. She was a welcome blessing to his eyes and was about to rush to her with joy, but a raised hand from Chief Nectowane paused him in his tracks. The woman was signalled by him to sit. She was offered water and food as she sat down and John sat, anxious to speak, but made mute by the protocol of the tribe. He waited. Outwardly calm, he hoped, but inwardly, impatient to speak.

Eventually, the ritual was complete and John was allowed to speak. The woman with the pale face, the colour of the moon, spoke with an accent John recognised - French.

'Dear Lady, my name is John. I have travelled a long way to meet with you. I have a great favour to ask. I know you have no reason to help me, but I beg of you... My wife...' John took a moment to compose himself, 'My wife, she is dying. She needs your help. It is said that you have a great medicine that can cure any illness - yes?' John spoke questioningly and looked hopefully towards the woman. The room was silent for a moment; deafeningly silent, waiting for this strange, unusually pale-skinned, woman to reply. It was the Chief Nectowance who responded next.

'Patience my son, this woman has been in deep meditation and should not have been disturbed. When she heard that a dark stranger had arrived she insisted she meet with you.' He bowed his head towards the woman, indicating with his hand that she could now speak.

'My name is Perenelle. I have been expecting you John.' Perenelle had turned towards John with a look of concern in her eyes. He had heard many interesting tales about people like Perenelle, people who 'knew' things before they had happened, but he had never before met anyone like her. John was disconcerted by her words. *How did she know his name or that he was coming to her?* He could only wonder. Normally, he would have asked questions, but he didn't have the time, he had to hurry to get back to his wife.

'Please... can you help?' John continued to describe the symptoms to Perenelle as quickly as he could, but it was as if she didn't need to be told.

'I need to return to my lodge where I have the potion already prepared for you, I have been waiting for you. I will be back shortly.' Perenelle graciously nodded at the weroance and waited for his nod of approval before standing up to leave. John waited nervously in silence. Chief Nectowane was a man of few words, but his eyes remained on John's face.

'May I see my horse?' he asked. The Chief once again signalled for one of the braves to take John to where his horse was being tended to. John was glad of the opportunity to get some fresh air into his lungs. The pipe smoke, the food smells, and the heat of the lodge, all left John feeling quite nauseous especially since he'd not had much sleep the night before, so he was glad of the respite.

The horse was in good condition. The young brave had fed and watered him, and left him in a shaded area on the edge of the camp. *Major would be refreshed for the return journey* was all John could think and was thankful to the brave. A squaw came over to John a short while later to take him back to the lodge. Perenelle was already sitting in the lodge with Chief Nectowance when John arrived. He was signalled by the Chief to be seated opposite the medicine woman. Formalities were carried out once again; Perenelle bowed to Chief Nectowane for permission to speak; he in turn indicated that she should speak directly to John.

'Take this potion to your wife. She must be given only a few drops in water every time she is given a drink, three or four times a day at least. She will be well in a few days. I have given you enough for your wife, your son, his family and yourself. Be well. May your journey home be a speedy one; but beware of crossing what looks like shallow water, especially in the dark as it could rise very quickly. There is danger if you do not heed me. You should use that time to rest 'til daybreak. Farewell my friend, and May your God go with you.' Then without further explanation she acknowledged the weroance, closing her eyes and bowing to him as she stood and turned to leave.

The Chief now speaking said simply -
'Your horse is ready. Food and water have been prepared for your journey. May your journey be a swift one' He signalled to a brave to take John outside. John turned to the chief and gratefully nodded before following the young brave outside.

The horse nickered softly, and John took in a deep breath of the cool, fresh air. It felt good filling his lungs, and he stroked the horse's muzzle reassuringly. All their supplies were loaded up, ready to leave.

John checked the horse's saddle bags and packages to make sure they were firmly secured. Then he caught the eye of the young brave who had cared for his horse and nodded his appreciation smiling. The boy stood back and bowed his head. His job was done.

John mounted his horse carefully so as not to startle him and made his way slowly through the village. Once at the edge of the camp he set off at a trot, then at full speed. Time was of the essence now. He prayed his luck would hold out; that he'd make good time. His thoughts were only on Ann...

Chapter Ten

The second time around

Hugh and Elizabeth sat up all night with Ann. She was feverish and restless, mumbling from time to time and calling John's name. The doctor had been called away to attend to other patients with the same sickness, which was running rampant through the plantations in Virginia. Before leaving, the doctor gave Elizabeth some instructions on how to care for Ann.

'Cover her up well we need to get her fever down. I know it's cold but we need to keep the windows open for fresh air to help with her breathing. Mop her brow regularly with a cold cloth; and if possible, try to get some fluids into her... at the very least, keep her lips moist... and', he paused momentarily before opening the door to leave, '... and pray!' he said solemnly closing the door hurriedly behind him."

It was clear that Ann was not doing well and Elizabeth went into her nursing mode without hesitation. She started attending to her patient as she had done for her aunt. Hugh smiled sadly at Elizabeth as she kept herself busy with different tasks. They had lost so many years together and he couldn't help but think about what could have been.

Hugh felt helpless sitting and only able to hold Ann's hand. He had felt this helpless before only twice in his life. The first time was when he almost lost his first wife during the birth of their second child. Ann had stepped in to help the local midwife deliver the baby and sent John to fetch the doctor after discovering that the child was the wrong way round and struggling to be born! Hugh's heart ached remembering how helpless he felt then and feeling it again now.

Despite being the master of the house, Hugh was not allowed in the bedroom whilst his wife was giving birth; so when a message was received instructing him to attend court, Hugh was glad of the distraction and left that morning unaware of the seriousness of his wife's condition. John ran as fast as he could to fetch the doctor that day, and although thoroughly exhausted, John continued to run to the courthouse to find the Hugh.

The second time was a few years later when his wife passed away a few years after she had their child. Her heart had been weak since the birth, and she was no longer able to fight. Hugh was totally distraught. It was the most he could do to get up in the morning. He was a broken man! It was John's forethought that came to the rescue on that occasion. He suggested advertising for help with their youngest child, The eldest, now full grown, was able to take care of himself, and help out on the plantation, but his youngest needed someone to care for him.

Hugh had been interviewing nannies all day when Elizabeth came in. He was exhausted and didn't even look up at her at first. Elizabeth was someone from his past who he never thought he would see again.

'Come in... come in.' He held his hand in the air waving it towards himself and indicating that the next applicant should sit down.

'Name?' Hugh asked wearily... No reply. The woman stood staring. Frozen to the spot as she saw the man... a few years older than when she last saw him, more than twenty years' ago, but it was definitely him!

'Name girl!' the man called, becoming irritated by the silence. He looked round, and there, standing before him was the woman he had loved and lost. The woman he had unexpectedly and inexplicably fallen in love with, one lonely night in Maryland. It was a night he never forgot.

Elizabeth approached Hugh shyly, unsure what to say next. Should she stay or should she go... Hugh stood up quickly... his heart beat so strong that he wondered if she could hear it! Momentarily he longed to rush to her and take her in his arms, but he stopped. It would be wrong. It would be inappropriate behaviour for a man of his stature; but the longing, the yearning... could she see it in his eyes? Did she feel what he was feeling..? With great difficulty Hugh took control of his burgeoning passions, reminding himself of his position; reminding himself why he was here... He shook Elizabeth's hand in greeting and led her to the chair assisting her to sit down then returned to his own place at the table and awkwardly began clearing his throat to speak.

Hugh was unsure if 'his' Elizabeth had recognized him. She made no outward sign of recognition other than the silence when she first entered the room. Demure and shyness were all he could discern from her manner. He decided it was best to continue the interview as normal to find out more about her, about what had become of her since last they'd seen one another.

Elizabeth needed a job. Her aunt had died leaving her only a small legacy in her will, which wouldn't last long. She thought she'd seen a glimmer of recognition in his face, but he didn't say as much. The interview went well. Elizabeth was quietly confident. She had experience in bringing up young children, omitting any explanation as to how, or whose children she had cared for, and Hugh didn't ask, for which she was thankful. She told him about her experience in caring for an elderly relative and managing a house, and knew she was more than capable of handling the job on offer. Should she remind Hugh of their acquaintance?

It was Hugh who first broached the subject on both their minds. He longed to take her in his arms and rekindle their passions, but Elizabeth gave him no indication that she even recognized him. He had discovered that she had not married. She had told him about living with her aunt for many years until she died. He needed to know if she remembered...

They discussed the post of 'nanny' for his child and if she felt she could run a home on a plantation away from the big city life that she had so obviously been used to, but in the end he felt he had to 'remind' her that they had met before... She admitted she knew who he was the moment she set eyes on him. She too longed to hold him close. It had been such a long time... but she held back... for she had a secret and didn't know if or how she should tell him. After both admitting they knew each other, Hugh ordered lunch for them both, they had much to talk about...

Minutes grew into hours. Day turned to night. Once their initial nervousness had gone, the shock at seeing one another again was behind them, it was as if they had never been parted. Time had passed so quickly for both Hugh and Elizabeth. Neither wanted to leave the other... His room was only a few steps away.

'Stay?' he asked Elizabeth, taking her hand in his and looking longingly, hopefully into her eyes... 'Don't go back to that empty house tonight. Stay with me?' squeezing her hands tenderly, he kissed them, a pleading look in his eyes. *How could she say no? She had loved him all these years. She'd refused to marry after their night together and especially after... How was she going to tell him? Should she stay, or should she go? One more night with the man she had loved all her life might be all she has left, once he knows she has a son... his son!* Elizabeth smiled a shy, embarrassed smile and nodded assent. Hugh's face lit up with pleasure and taking her hand he stood up. Elizabeth turned to pick up her bags before standing, but Hugh took them from her and led her through the foyer, stopping momentarily to speak with the receptionist where he ordered drinks and a light supper to be brought to his room. As Elizabeth stood alone waiting for his return, she began to have doubts, almost running away, embarrassed. Hugh returned just as she was about to leave, she caught sight of his smiling face, the face she had held in her memory all those years. Her doubts left her as Hugh took her hand in his, kissing it so gently, and as old as she now was, it was like all the years melted away, she felt young again! Hugh guided her up the stairs. She followed willingly, an overwhelming sense of excitement and anticipation ran through her body; what lay ahead she wasn't altogether sure, for Hugh had always been a gentleman even after they'd spent that night together all those years ago, he had never made her feel less than a lady. Whatever was about to happen she knew it was what she wanted; she was sure it would be a night to remember.

Chapter Eleven

John – the return journey

John had been trying to make up for lost time. He was riding the horse fast, but as daylight began to fade and he was nearing a river he'd have to cross, he decided, reluctantly, it would be safest to camp for the night and start afresh in the morning.

The river was tidal. It ebbed and flowed with the motions of the sea it came from and although the tide was low right now it would come in fast once the tide turned. The crossing was wide and would be unsafe in the dark; *besides* he reasoned to himself, *most of his day was spent at the Indian camp, at least he'd got what he came for he'd start anew at daybreak. By then the tide should be low enough to cross before it turns again... he would be able to make better time at least that was his hope.*

John found a suitable spot not too far from the riverbank, yet sufficient protection from the elements with the trees nearby

'Good kindling for the fire tonight boy... should be nice and warm 'til morning' he told Major.

The Powhatan's had been very kind and generous. They not only gave John enough food to help him reach home, but they also gave him a bottle of their home-brewed wine and an extra blanket. This was an incredible act of kindness and one that John would always remember.

'This should definitely help keep out the cold' he told his horse and laughed.

John was already showing signs of exhaustion as he gathered kindling, but setting a fire and putting a pot of water on to boil had to be his first priority. He could attend to the horse while it boiled. As hungry as he was, he found it difficult to do more than nibble at the food that his earlier generous hosts had given him. *A beaker of wine might help he thought.* Forcing himself to nibble on the food and drink some wine, he settled himself down to sleep. He collapsed exhausted near the fire, but as much as he tried, his mind wouldn't let him sleep. He sat up and pulled his blanket about him and looked out across the river. The tide was out at the moment, *it had become shallow enough to cross*, he thought, then common sense took over. Major had kept going, but like himself, the horse was in need of rest. He watched the movement of the water to gauge how long it would take for the tide to turn. He wondered how long he would have to cross the wide expanse of water in daylight. He'd have to time it right. They had to be careful. The moon was bright and the sky was clear. His restless time wouldn't be wasted. Timing would be crucial, but they'd crossed the river once on the way up, they could do it again, then he remembered Perenelle's warning, some sort of danger and something about water… doubt crossed him mind fleetingly *then maybe not!*

Looking out across the water, John could just imagine the spirits that Indians spoke of, watching over him. He'd heard talk about the spirits they believed in helping those in need if they were true in their heart. John wondered if his love for Ann would be seen as true? Ann... He hoped and prayed with all his heart that he would be in time to save her, that the potion Perenelle gave him would work... He had to believe. He had to be strong - for Ann!

As clouds intermittently hid the moon and the night grew dark, the air began to cool. John was glad he found the extra blanket in his bed-roll. He wondered if it had been added by one of the squaws on instructions from Perenelle. She was a strange woman, an enigma. She seemed to know who he was - she had been 'expecting' him she said, but how?

Is it truly possible to know things in advance, to know people you have never met? Whatever her story, she was good. John could almost 'feel' a serenity that emanated from her. He closed his eyes, dwelling on her face for a moment, seeing her image in his mind's eye. At first, she was looking down, her eyes almost closed then suddenly they opened, frightening John so much he jumped back. *He must have been drifting off to sleep,* he rationalized, dreaming or something for suddenly he was awake!

Looking around, he saw eyes staring at him, low to the ground. Then a low hiss in the direction of his horse... John reached for the shotgun he'd never thought he'd have to use, and grabbed a chunk of wood lighting it from the dying fire. Slowly he walked toward his horse speaking in a quiet calming tone as the horse began to whinny, sensing danger. He moved his arm holding the firewood in the direction of the eyes to frighten the creature away, whatever it was and fired a warning shot. A second shot and he heard a crack as the bullet hit a tree branch causing it to fall. Hissing could be heard and a rattling sound. John threw out his arm that held the fire stick in an attempt to frighten away whatever was causing the sound to keep it away from the horse, then in the light from the fire he saw what looked like two snakes close together and he let off a shot hoping to kill at least one of them and frighten the other away. The sound stopped. John rushed to his horse to calm him before untying and walking him nearer to the fire; grabbing kindle on his way. The fire needed to be maintained to keep more of whatever was out there from coming close. The sudden rush of adrenalin was now leaving him and with it a sensation of fatigue. Securing his horse a little closer, John lay down once more feeling exhausted and fell into a fitful sleep.

Chapter Twelve

Elizabeth is struggling

Elizabeth was getting worried it had been a day and a half since she'd sent for their son, the only reverend for miles around. Ann was becoming weaker.

'Dear God' she prayed, 'Let her live a little longer, at least until her husband returns or Reverend John arrives.' Elizabeth had stopped being religious years ago, but she had seen how much Ann's faith meant to her, especially these past few years.

Annoyed, frustrated, angry... she looked over at Hugh; he had fallen asleep again. Even though she knew he was just as exhausted as she was, she couldn't help but feel angry at him. Didn't he know this was as hard on her as it was on him? She'd already seen enough death in her life losing her father and eldest brother to the warring Indians. Hugh was all she had left now, and she needed him to be awake and alert. *Thank goodness we're at peace with the Indians at the moment, especially now, when John needs to find his miracle woman, this potion peddler!* Elizabeth wasn't so good at believing in miracles; especially after caring for her aunt.

Her aunt had been at death's door several times before she finally found blessed peace. Every time she was near death or took a turn for the worst, Elizabeth would send for the doctor and he'd tell her how close her aunt was to 'meeting her maker', and every time she would have to call her family; the very same family who had disowned her for refusing to marry; the very same family who wanted nothing to do with her when she was with child!. And every time, by some 'miracle' they called it, her aunt would revive! Each time a little weaker than the last, but alive all the same... it was as if she had nine lives. 'She's just like a cat' her youngest brother joked, but it was no joke when you had to live with her, getting meaner and more feeble by the hour!

The doctor explained that her anger was a result of her mental state; she was battling the desire to end her life along with the fear of dying. It caused her to act irrationally they said. Elizabeth felt helpless; she didn't want her aunt to die, but she also didn't want her to keep suffering. She was reliving all the negative emotions she felt when she watched her aunt go through this process; the feeling of helplessness, the watching, waiting, nursing, tending to Ann... it brought back all those feelings, and all Hugh could do was sleep!!

As if sensing something amiss, Hugh suddenly roused, *or was it the bowl of water that Elizabeth accidentally spilled over his knees as she'd passed him...* she wondered.

'Aahh... aahh... cold! What...?' shouted Hugh with annoyance, then apologizing for shouting when he realized where he was.

'Have I been asleep long?' he asked brushing away the water, trying to shake his trousers dry. 'Is there any news of John yet? What about the reverend?'

'You've slept most of the night' said Elizabeth irritated, but passive and exhausted. 'I've been able to keep her cool. She's taken a few sips of water as the doctor suggested. Can you take over for a while I sort out some food? We need to eat if we're to keep vigil over Ann.' Elizabeth needed a break. She needed to get away from these feelings that were churning up inside, feelings she'd thought she'd left behind her, but they weren't. Grief; she'd never been able to handle it. She had to get away!

Hugh

Hugh lit his pipe. Ann was asleep. Then realizing that his smoke might aggravate her breathing he walked to the door to watch the sunrise... the dawn of a new day. *Nothing changed* he thought. *Life goes on as normal as if nothing was happening of any importance other than a new day. Nature was a cruel, unfeeling mother at times, but looking at the rising of the sun... he had to admit, it gave hope.*

As he smoked his pipe he remembered the day John came to him asking for his permission to marry Ann. John had been working with Hugh as his assistant for a few months by that time. Mary-Anne, his housekeeper, had brought John to his attention.

It must have been around the time Ann was his scullery maid he remembered. Mary-Anne told him about this young, educated, black man who had travelled from England to be an indentured servant.

'He is smart and a hard worker' she'd told him.

Hugh had been intrigued by her account. It was rare for Mary-Anne to speak so highly of someone. He was impressed.

'He speaks excellent English for a foreigner' she said 'brought up with a troupe of travelling actors or something to all accounts.'

John had a great gift for communication. He was always able to find a way to understand what people were saying, and make himself understood, no matter where they were from or what language they spoke. He could talk to anyone, and his openness and warmth always made people feel at ease.

'He would be an asset' she suggested in her matter-of-fact way. Mary-Anne had always had a special place in Hugh's heart. She was like a mother to him for years before his first wife, came over to America with their son.

After giving John a few simple tasks to see how he got on, it wasn't long before Hugh took him on full-time as his personal assistant. It was a huge undertaking. Hugh had just become Justice of the Peace for York County and was in need of someone he could trust, with a good head on his shoulders and a way with people, to help with his paperwork. John was good with people and honest, and Hugh felt he could be trusted to take legal documents to Maryland, to the Assembly.

In all their years together, there had been only one problem, well quite a serious problem, which could have cost him the friendship with John that he now enjoys...

He'd been called to the court in Maryland to sign papers for the patent for 1000 acres of land on the island he was now living... A few years earlier, when he was young, long before he was the Burgess for the House of Charles County, he had saved a young Indian girl from drowning. She'd turned out to be the daughter of a local Chief. Out of gratitude, after her father died, she gave Hugh a whole island as thanks. Hugh accepted the island in the King's name. Later on he asked if he could be granted a portion of the land to distribute amongst his indentured servants whose indentures were nearing an end. As a rule, Hugh would have told John about his business in Maryland, but he hadn't intended being away too long, and John was working elsewhere, he never got round to tell John about it. In hindsight, he wished he had done so, for John was almost branded or worse still killed – as a runaway! Hugh's train of thought was cut short when he heard a commotion a short distance away... it was his son, Reverend John arriving.

Chapter Thirteen

John – One night down, two more to go

John woke up the next morning to darkness. He'd finally fallen asleep but was now so hungry he could've eaten a bear! The dying embers of the fire were all that was left to see by. The moon that was full just a few hours ago was now low in the sky, hidden behind dark clouds that gave no light. John had left some kindling nearby for morning, so it wasn't long before he was enjoying the welcoming warmth of a good fire. It would be a while yet before it was light enough to begin his journey. John tended to his horse, put water over the fire to boil, and checked on the river's flow. It was on the ebb. Currents would be a little strong to begin with, always at their strongest on the turn of the tide. There would be time to eat. The fire warmed him right through to the bones. The breakfast and hot beverage nourished him from within.

He was ready to begin his journey when he suddenly remembered the creature he had shot the previous night. He was curious to discover what it was, and almost laughed with fear when he found what appeared to be a two-headed snake. He poked at the creature carefully, curious. He'd never seen a snake with two heads before. His grandson would be fascinated by it. John decided to take it back to show him. He'd heard its rattle, so guessed it could be poisonous. Would it be worth the danger to see the look on his face, or Ann's for that matter, he wondered? Using a two-pronged stick he'd found in the brush, he picked up the snake and smiled at the thought of his family's faces when he got home. He stopped. For a moment he'd forgotten how seriously ill his wife was. For a moment he'd been thinking of the future, for a moment...

John was filled with guilt, brought back to reality with a sudden thump in his chest as he remembered. The smile that he wore, for just a moment, was suddenly gone, replaced by a look of anguish at his thoughtlessness.

He had to hurry. There was no time to waste. Fastening and securing the snake in, what was thought to be, a now empty saddle bag which had once contained food packed by the Indians, he put out the fire, packed away his equipment and set off on the second leg of his journey in a slightly more subdued manner. He'd almost forgotten... just for a moment, and he felt guilty. What was he thinking? He's not out on a jaunty ride? He was on a mission to save his wife! He had a long way still to go. He hoped to reach Topahanocke and find shelter before nightfall.

The tide had changed, and the river was low enough for him to cross safely. He'd heard stories about monsters who lived in the river. Remembering Perenelle's warning about the dangers of water, he hoped the two-headed snake was the only thing he had to worry about.

The river crossing was quite cold, both in the air and in the water. Despite the low tide, there was still at least a foot of water to wade through. With riverbed creatures wriggling under foot, Major stepped as carefully and sure-footedly as he could. Fortunately, this smaller section of the river passed without serious incident. Major whinnied once or twice as river creatures occasionally touched his fetlocks, but he remained firm and steadfast. John was thankful to have such a sturdy creature for his companion.

By the time they reached dry land, it was almost noon. John wanted to keep going, but after the cold crossing, they both needed warmth. It was a fair distance before they reached a suitable resting place to build a fire. John's mind had been filled with concerns for their safety. He'd heard that the river at this point occasionally had sharks and although they usually only appeared during high tides, they had been known to be stranded in shallow water which made them dangerous. He was relieved that the immediate danger was over and was able to think of Ann once again and for the first time in his life he found himself praying –

'Dear Lord, I know you don't know me. I know you have no reason to listen to me, but my Ann, she has been a loyal servant to your all of her life. Please... I ask this not for myself alone, but for my son, let Ann live. Help me to reach her with this medicine in time. I promise... if you will allow me this one request, I will pray alongside Ann whenever she prays... I will attend a service whenever a priest comes. I promise you Lord whatever you want, just, please... Let my Ann live? Ann's only sin has been not be able to be married in your sight. I know that's been partly my fault, but if you'll let her live, I promise I'll get baptised, I'll do whatever she wants, whatever it takes, but please I beg you – let her live?'

John pleaded with a God he'd never believed in. He'd never found the need. Life was life and he lived it the best he could. His mother had never forced him, or his brother, to go to church. She, herself, had fallen out with her God a long time ago. She blamed him for taking her mother away from her when she was young. John had always wondered what the fuss was about, but not enough to get churched, but Ann was different. Her faith was everything to her. She'd been a good wife, a good mother. In the absence of a preacher, Hugh, as the owner of their indentures and Justice of the Peace, had performed their marriage ceremony. Hugh... he'd become a good friend to him... to them both in fact. There was only that one time... John paused, refusing to dwell on bad memories from the past.

He had finally reached a good spot to rest. He built a fire and put some water on the fire to make a hot drink before resuming his journey. Leaving the horse to graze he ate and drank a little of the food, warming himself by the fire with a hot drink. He began to feel angry at himself as he sat staring into the fire. What right did he have to try to bribe God, if there even was such a thing? He shook his head helplessly.

He remembered the last time he'd tried to do the right thing by Ann. It was when their son was about three years of age. He had so much on his mind. His indentures would soon be ending. Master Hugh had gone on business to Maryland and didn't say when he'd be back. He'd heard some exciting news about a Jesuit priest who had bought some land just south of Maryland. He was building a Manse where all clergy from thereabouts could stay. He was also looking for reliable, hardworking tenant farmers to let the land to; people whose indentures were ending. He and Ann... they could have their own piece of farmland – John was excited, he wanted in. He wanted to put his name down for a farm and while he was speaking to him he wanted to ask the priest to baptize him. On top of that, in order to make Ann happy, he wanted to ask the Father to marry them - he was so excited about his plan! The only problem was - he needed permission from Master Hugh.

Hugh had said he was going to be in Maryland on business. John was sure he'd be easy to find, everyone knew Master Hugh. In John's head, he would find Master Hugh, get his permission to be baptized and marry, then head on up to see the Father with an appropriate letter from Master Hugh that would authorise him to do the journey. Plus… it was make a lovely surprise for Ann! It all sounded so simple… in John's head.

Unfortunately, fate was not on his side. He didn't have permission to be off the plantation and two other servants, James and Victor, had the same idea… that of leaving the plantation without permission. He argued with them to go back to the plantation. He told them they'd be in trouble for leaving the plantation without permission, but they wouldn't listen! They followed John and no matter what he said, they wouldn't go back. John wasn't happy, but there was no use arguing with them. He had a long way to go. Maryland was at least a two or three day walk if he didn't waste time. He only hoped that three people walking together wouldn't bring them unwanted attention. Hugh would for sure, be all right with giving John his permission to leave once he knew the reason for sure, but two others…? He'd be livid! It was expecting too much, he felt anxious having others with him, he realised then, just how much of a risk he was taking. He was having second thoughts, but it was too dark to turn back. He decided to wait 'til morning.

The journey had been slow. The roads were treacherously dangerous due to the flash lightning storm they'd experienced. The heavy rain made finding shelter a matter of urgency. Fortunately, John remembered a dilapidated old barn he'd seen on one of his previous trips to Maryland. It was still there, but barely standing. *Definitely abandoned and would give the three of them a modicum of shelter for the night at least* thought John.

James and Victor had not planned their journey well. They had only a few pieces of dried bread and some home-brewed beer they'd stolen from the masters' kitchens. *Another reason for the master to be furious when he found out*, thought John. He didn't have time to worry about that now. Eat, sleep and hopefully be dry by morning was the only thing on John's mind as he fell exhausted into a deep dreamless sleep.

James and Victor were still arguing the next day. They wouldn't make up their minds in which direction they were going. John tried to talk them into going back with him before anyone had the chance to notice they were gone, but they were having none of it! Irritated, John set off in the direction of the plantation, hoping they would follow. The other two set off in the opposite direction. All of a sudden there was a lot of shouting coming from the direction of James and Victor, John ran to see if he could help, when suddenly he himself was surrounded, men shouting and grabbing at him without question. His arms and legs were bound and he was thrown onto a waggon that seemed to appear from nowhere, with James and Victor already on it. John had no idea who they were or where they were being taken. There were just lots of shouting and muttering to be heard some distance ahead and shots were fired into the air, as if signalling someone. *What was happening?* John wondered. Hugh will sort it out... if only he can get word to him, but where were they being taken to and on whose authority? John had worked with Hugh long enough to know that you don't just get accosted like this without just cause.

Chapter Fourteen

The arrival of Reverend John

Hugh was so relieved to see his son again. A great deal of time had passed since they'd last met and they had not parted on good terms. He hoped they could overcome their differences, for Ann's sake.

Ann and John had been good to his son after his mother died. He was a young man with issues which he carried with him to this day... or hopefully, maybe... not. When his mother almost died giving birth to his brother Richard, he hated the baby. Ann and John were the only people he'd listen to. Hugh had always felt guilty for not being around when Richard was born but he'd been called away on Burgess' business rushing back as soon as John reached him with the news that his wife was in labour and struggling with the birth. John had ran all the way, to find him. That was to be the start of their friendship, Ann played her part too she'd stay with his wife the whole time, helping to nurse her until he could return. There was so much for which he had to thank John and Ann.

Hugh gazed at his son with immense pride - Reverend John! His son was animatedly talking with his stepmother Elizabeth. Although they hadn't taken to each other as quickly as he'd hoped. His youngest Richard had fallen in love with her straight away! Hugh admitted he did remarry a little more quickly than was socially acceptable, but he had never expected to see Elizabeth again - the love of his life. He couldn't let her slip through his fingers a second time!

'It's too soon. Have you no respect for mother?' His eldest son had almost screamed at him in a fit of rage!

It was just one more reason for his son's resentment. Hugh cringed at the memory. So much had happened between them. So much they never talked about.

Hugh couldn't let his private thoughts impinge on what needed to be done now. The focus had to be on Ann, what 'she' needed, and there wasn't much time. She was hanging on to life, *just waiting for her husband to return*, thought Hugh. *Let him return soon*, Hugh silently prayed.

Elizabeth greeted Reverend John in her usual way with food and drink. *She must have Indian blood in her*, Hugh smiled to himself; for he'd noticed how she always had to provide visitors with nourishment, even before they had time to sit and talk. He smiled as he watched Elizabeth fussing over their new guest. He really didn't know what he would do without her. *I really should tell her more often just how much he appreciated her*, he thought.

Suddenly Elizabeth was disturbed from her usual hospitality as Ann began to heave again. There was nothing more to come out of her, but every heave weakened her further and she'd been dry-heaving for hours! Elizabeth tried lifting Ann up to help her swallow. She'd tried soup, tea, coffee and they'd all come back up. So having prepared some cool boiled water this time and adding lemon she was able to trickle the liquid between her lips, hoping that some might go down her throat.

The reverend had barely partaken of his own refreshment, before he began praying cleansing and blessing the home. Looking round the room he caught sight of his father. Without acknowledgment, he paused, and continued his ritual, blessing everyone in the room, offering pleas for protection for all those present; never once mentioning anyone by name. He prayed to remove evil and negative influences, *but how can he clearing such influences when he still appeared angry at his father*, Hugh wondered cynically. Reverend John continued going about his ritual unperturbed by his father's presence.

Taking Ann's hands, he prayed for her soul; prayed that her suffering be brought to an end, for her to get well... or be given absolution for her sins - and peace. The reverend hated this part. The sense of futility, helplessness - it never got any easier. He'd seen so many deaths since starting his ministry that he'd learned to harden himself to grief. No one knew exactly what was killing all these people. Some said it was the water that was contaminated; others said it was a plague on all evil wrong-doers, but what had Ann done that was so wrong? She hadn't an evil bone in her body! He'd known her for much of his life. She'd helped his mother when her end was near. She had been a strong influence on him and probably one of the reasons he had taken up the church. She and John had shown him so much kindness, especially after his father came back with a new wife! *No negative influences* he told himself repeatedly, regrouping his thoughts to focus on

Ann. Right now he had to do what he could for her... She needed absolution for her sins and he knew that Ann had always felt like a sinner. For years, she'd lived in a state of mortal sin. She'd never been married in the eyes of her God.

'Dear God, if there is one thing I can do for this woman that will give her peace then please, allow me this, to bring her peace. Give her time. Allow her to see her John once more. Allow me the honour of marrying her to the man she loves, in the eyes of you Lord. Dear God... let me be your agent and bless this woman and her family before you take her.' Reverend John prayed with all his intent to be able to do the right thing. Holding Ann's hand; sitting in silent prayer with his head bowed. He watched and waited for his miracle. Hugh watched his son. *Everything would be good from now on – he knew it, he felt it!*

Chapter Fifteen

John – Almost home

The night was drawing in, it was getting late. The township of Topahanocke could be seen on the horizon. 'We're close to town now boy' he told Major, 'then we can rest.' He'd felt guilty for taking longer than intended, after the last river crossing, *if only he hadn't momentarily closed his eyes* - he scolded himself. He'd planned on finding shelter, outside of town, before the storm, that had been brewing overhead, finally broke. He knew it wouldn't be safe to stay in town because of the troubles they'd had with the Rappahannock tribe, and with the colour of his skin, at night... there could be trouble.

He'd heard through his contacts at court that the Rappahannock tribe had sold Topahanocke to some colonists, but after settling, the colonists refused to pay and the Indians wouldn't wait for the courts to resolve the matter, preferring to take matters into their own hands, they ransacked the town at every opportunity. John hoped that at least tonight would be peaceful - he was exhausted!

Storm clouds had been gathering from the east and the air smelled like rain. He saw what looked like a dilapidated old barn just beyond the entrance to the town and set his horse on a final gallop hoping to make the distance before the storm broke.

A partially broken water-barrel stood near the door, John noticed as they arrived, hopefully it would still contain fresh rain water. As they entered the building John almost fell off his horse with exhaustion. Despite tiredness John's first priority was to the horse. Unsaddling and dropping the packages to the floor to allow the horse to rest. He found an empty stall containing hay and placed Major inside to eat. A bucket was hanging nearby, undamaged and John filled it with water from the barrel and topped up his water pouches for the next day while he could still move.

Overcome by fatigue John grabbed what was left of the food and a blanket to wrap round him and fell asleep. *'Only one more day to go'* he told himself, *'only one more day to go…*

'A good nights' sleep, that's all we need boy… We'll manage - we have to.'

His thoughts were on Ann as he fell asleep. They'd been together for more than twenty years, and although times were hard for everyone, John felt blessed to have shared his life with Ann. She had been his rock. When John had been taken by the sheriff's men years earlier, their son was only young. He thought he'd never see them again, but then Master Hugh came through for him. The Governor dealt his punishment believing John a runaway. Thirty lashes they'd all been given… thirty lashes… each! Victor and James were indeed running away; their punishment was Just, but John had been trying to do the right thing in the end, he'd been trying to get them to go back. It wasn't fair. It was the one thing he'd found hard to forgive at the time, but all was well in the end, once he knew the truth.

Chapter Sixteen

Elizabeth – It's all too much to bear!

Once Elizabeth was happy that Ann was settled once again, she busied herself once again sorting refreshments for their guest. Reverend John had always shown her politeness and respect, but she was aware that she did not meet with his approval although he blamed his father more than he did herself. Either way, she knew that Hugh and his son needed to talk. The tension between them was, to Elizabeth, so apparent, or maybe it was something else she was feeling. Whatever it was, she had to make an exit. She told the two men that she would organize food and drink to be brought to the hut, but in reality, Elizabeth needed an escape. She needed to get out of the room.

Elizabeth was struggling on two levels. One, she had never been good at handling death. The living, the nursing, she could cope with, but the closer death came, the more distance she needed from it; and two – see Hugh with his son reminder her of her own son, Jack.

Jack was her pet name for him. He'd been baptized John Gwynn Fielding. He was the son she'd had after her liaison with Hugh and even now, she had never dared to tell him. Even now, when he was her husband, she was afraid of how he would react and the longer she put it off, the harder it got.

She'd not seen Jack for years, didn't know if he was dead or alive… Not since she'd had a blazing row with her parents about him. Her parents had been dictating their Last Will and Testament to a lawyer, favouring her sibling's children over her own son. She hadn't heard him enter the room, not until her father stopped in his tracks after yelling –

'He's *your* bastard son! Let his father take care of him when he dies..!'
In that instant, her father tried to apologize to Jack, but it was too late! The look of surprise, shock, disgust, disbelief all those things crossed her sons face. He said nothing as he turned to leave. Grabbing his arm, pleading with him not to go, he just ran – to where, she didn't know. Her last memory of him was seeing that look of disgust on his face as he pulled away from her. It was a look she didn't want to see on her husband's face.

She rationalized over the years that it was her own fault. Her parents had accepted him as one of their own. It was her own stubbornness that made her insist that he knew she was his mother. She'd always told him that his father had been killed at the hands of the Indians… That he was borne out of love before they could marry. She's brought it all on herself with her stupid pride. Jack was an innocent. He was all she had left of the man she loved.

Despite knowing Hugh for such a short time, their journey into the city and the one night they had together, she had loved him a lifetime. She'd lived all her life without him. She's cared for and raised his son in the best way she could, given him the best education she could. Jack was her life. He was all that kept her going through the years of looking after her thankless, belligerent old aunt.

Her aunt had not spoken a single word of kindness to her in all their time together, not a single word unless it was to scold or demand attendance. Jack was her comfort. He would be her solace after a difficult day with her aunt. She loved listening to his childish chatter. He'd talk about everything he'd done that day. Tell her what he'd learnt. He was always so full of excitement about everything he did! He was a blessing to her and they had each other.

A few years after he'd left, word did reach her that Jack had been seen a few towns away. The wife of a local trader, a woman known for her love of gossip, told her he was travelling with the trader who used to sell hardware in their own town. He'd changed his name, dropping the name of *Fielding so as not to be associated with his old life*, she added. The woman spoke with such relish as she almost gloated over her news to Elizabeth.

Elizabeth was left heartbroken. It had been bad enough her parents dismissing her when they sent her to live with her aunt, but to hear that her own son wanted to disown even knowing her - it was unbearable! She'd loved that child all his life unconditionally. She'd given up her life to keep, to feed and clothe him. He'd been her strength.

Seeing Reverend John... The memory of those times gone past... watching Ann dying, it was all too much. Tears she'd held back for years all came flooding out as she walked to the house. Alice rushed to her when she noticed the tears, but all Elizabeth could do was nod and shake her head as she asked questions about Ann. Signalling the need for food and drink to be taken over to Hugh was the best she could do before taking to her room to compose herself.

Chapter Seventeen

Hugh

Hugh looked on as his son John *'the reverend'* busied himself preparing to give Ann her last rites. She had been in and out of consciousness most of the day. *What use is it to force a dying woman to eat bread when she can barely swallow,* thought Hugh, disdainfully? As proud as he was of his son's achievement, his own anger towards a God who could let his wife die…

He was reminded of the death of his first wife. Hugh had prayed… begged and even pleaded for his wife to live, but his words went unheeded. He'd become very angry, blamed himself for not being with her when their son was born. Their youngest had been a difficult birth and Ann. The strain had left her with a weakened heart from which she never fully recovered. After she died, Hugh lost his faith in God for a long time; leaving him a widower with a young child to bring up. John and Ann had done what they could to help, but instead of being thankful for any help he was offered, he chose to push people away instead. He didn't want pity, he wanted his wife!

His eldest had handled his mother's death quite differently. He found his faith, even thanking God for freeing her from her earthly body, freeing her from her suffering! But Hugh needed her… he needed his wife and their youngest needed his mother.

As he sat watching his son unpack his paraphernalia, Hugh began to realise how selfish he had been. Reverend John took every artefact from him bag, blessed them and placed them carefully, reverently around Ann's bed: a bible, old and battered, he kissed and blessed; a wooden crucifix that had seen better days, kissed and blessed; a chalice, a half-empty bottle of wine and Holy water duly blessed and set to one side... he added one or two of Ann's personal items and placed them carefully about her. He asked for bread to be brought over... Elizabeth had already pre-empted his needs, asking Alice to set aside extra bread for the communion when she brought the food for them all.

Hugh had never understood why his son did what he did. He had been furious! They'd quarrelled when his son told him his intentions. He couldn't understand how his son could be so forgiving of a God who took the life of his mother! They'd never discussed his decision. Hugh had just shouted wildly at his son and he left the house without his blessing. They'd not spoken since. Not seen one another – until now!

Hugh could see Ann was sinking away fast. And as he watched his son work, despite himself, he began to pray, to whom? He wasn't sure. To Ann... *for* Ann, he wasn't sure, maybe... Maybe his prayers would be heard this time - by God:

'Hold on Ann... John is on his way.'

Chapter Eighteen

Topahanocke Rampaged

It was still dark when John was woken abruptly by loud, ear-shattering war cries. John had heard the sounds before when Indians were on the rampage. A shrieking owl-like sound as they charged towards their foe. The suddenness of the sounds frightened the horse. He whinnied and neighed with fright, his hooves clambering to escape his stall. John ran to calm him. He had to stop any sound. Grabbing the reins and pulling his head down towards him, talking soothingly all the time 'til he could reach and stroke his muzzle, it was all he could do. Hopefully they were far enough away from the main entrance of the town, not to be in any immediate danger of being heard a stray scout wandering close by could be their only worry.

Screams and shouts sounded from the village, lots of clashing and yelling. The sky was brightly lit from buildings that had been set on fire. Horses were running wildly with fear, out of their enclosures. Men and women were either chasing after horses or heaving buckets of water to put out the flames.

John's first instinct was to run and help, but as he looked through broken wooden slats in the barn wall, he saw Indians on horses now leaving the cacophony of sound with whoops of joy on a successful raid. The hoard of Indians left as quickly as they'd arrived. John looked on, troubled by indecision. Reluctantly, and against his basic instinct, he decided not to get involved...

Angry villagers might mistake him for one of the warriors, a chance he couldn't take. There could only be one thing on his mind right now and that was to get back to Ann.

The sun rose slowly, casting an eerie glow on the scene of destruction before him. John felt a sense of helplessness, but his obligation to his wife was stronger. She was his priority. He must prepare and re-pack the horse before setting off. There should be one more day to go, he reminded himself. With renewed resolve, John hurriedly gobbled down the last of his provisions and set off once again on the last haul of their journey. *Almost at an end, boy* he patted Major *almost at an end...* he hoped, not knowing how much time he had left - there was no time to waste was all he truly knew.

'Dear Lord... it's me again' John closed his eye after mounting the horse and spoke aloud. 'Please... Give me strength, and swiftness of foot to this wonderful, brave horse.' He patted Major on the neck. 'Keep Ann alive. Let this potion work. Don't let the journey be in vain. Let her live, Lord. I beg you... we need just a little more time - please!'

Chapter Nineteen

There's travellers ahead

Sun was setting as John approached the mouth of the Piankatank River. He was weak and tired from hunger, having eaten the last of their provisions hours before.

'Not much further' he told Major, pausing to consider the next problem ahead of them, a narrow stretch of water between the mainland and the island. John had left his boat moored on the riverbank. If it wasn't there it probably meant it had been used by the reverend – he hoped he was wrong. If it wasn't there, they'd both have to swim for it! The water would be cold, he wasn't getting any younger and he was tired.

'We'll tackle that problem when we get there, won't we boy?' He addressed the horse aloud. 'Only a few miles left… Oh, Lord, help us.'

John had never prayed before, yet this journey had been challenging. Was there a God? Was there someone to hear his prayers, or was he talking to himself? All John could think was – HELP!

The moon was on the wane, but still almost full, sufficient light to see by provided they moved slowly and carefully. He saw a light moving towards them, it was a waggon. As it neared, he could just make out its outline, it was one of those trading waggons, with pots, pans and a sundry of other goods hanging all over. *Probably on its way to market* he guessed, his mind beginning to wander with fatigue.

'Hi there stranger,' greeted the driver as their paths met, 'where're you off to at this time of night?'

John rode alongside the waggon, to answer the stranger's question. To be honest, it had been a long lonely journey, he was tired of hearing his own voice. It was good to hear someone else for a change.

'I have to get across the river to that island over there,' replied John pointing towards the river and Gwynn's Island. 'My wife is dying. I was told a medicine woman staying with Indians in the north could work miracles. She gave me a potion, I have to get to my wife tonight!' he told the stranger, pointing behind him to the north and to the east where he was now heading.

'Have you come far, yourself?' asked John by way of conversation.

'Mathews' replied the driver looking over his shoulder from where he'd come. 'We were just about to set up camp.'

John noticed then, a woman sitting beside the driver, a baby in her arms, and both were wrapped in a blanket.

'I know you're in a hurry, but it's too dark to be crossing any water even in this moonlight. Besides, you and your horse both look mighty weary, it wouldn't be safe. Why don't you join us, stay awhile. You're welcome to share our supplies, and the good woman here... she can whip up a mighty tasty meal from practically nothing, she can.' He invited John to stay, winking proudly at his wife. 'I tell you what' he continued. 'Stay with us the night and we'll help you cross the river – together - tomorrow. We're always on the lookout for new customers willing to part with their money' he winked and laughed, rolling around in his seat. 'I'll help you and you'll help me. How's that suit ya?'

'I really can't spare the t...' time, John was about to say, shaking his head, but was interrupted by the new acquaintance

'We won't take no for an answer... will we Janey' said the stranger smiling at his wife.

John was silent for a while, pondering the invitation. On one hand he needed to get back to Ann urgently; on the other... the river would be cold, he and the horse *were* both weary, and in need of sustenance. They could do with the rest. As they approached the river, his new friend came to a halt and dismounted. John struggled with indecision, but in the end the traveller talked sense. What good would he be to Ann if he tried swimming in the dark, got cramp with the cold, and drowned? The final clincher was the rumble of his stomach and the whinny of the horse, decision was made; stay and enjoy a welcome and unexpected repast with these fine people and start afresh in the morning.

There wasn't going to be much sleep with a baby crying off and on through the night, but John had enjoyed chatting with his new found friend. The man was called John as well,

'...but my friends call me Jack' he said. His wife was Jane, and the baby was Lilibet,

'... named after my mother, Elizabeth' he told John. 'She doesn't even know I'm married, let alone have a child.' He paused as he reminisced. 'Mother loves children,' he said almost to himself and pausing... Then as if remembering he had a guest he resumed more chattily. 'She'd be over the moon if she knew about the baby. Sad thing is we quarrelled, a long time ago. I left home without as much as a goodbye and haven't seen her since. Then I met my Janie...' he looked over to where his wife lay with their daughter. 'We met and married in all of six weeks. I knew the first time I set eyes on her that she was right woman for me.' He smiled again in the direction of his wife. As there was nothing else to do, Jack continued telling his story:

'We went back home to see my Ma, but she wasn't there. She'd gone. No one seemed to know where, and no one seemed to care, either. We'd always kept ourselves to ourselves you see.' Jack went quiet. He stared into the fire, a lost look on his face as if he wanted to say more, but for some reason chose to hold his tongue.

John looked across at Jack a look of empathy as he thought of his own mother back home in England. He missed her. He missed all his family, his father and brother too. He'd not quarrelled with them like Jack, but his mother hadn't wanted him to travel to the new world. He'd left anyway - *to follow his dreams of adventure.* Despite her own misgivings about losing her son, his mother had waved him off with a smile on her face. She could always be seen with a smile on her face, even when times were hard. She would encourage people to follow their dreams even though she had lost sight of many of her own.

Occasionally, John felt guilty for leaving her, but he knew in his heart that his mother would have wanted him to live his dream! He pondered a while on his family. They'd welcomed him with open arms, once Master William had used his power of persuasion on them with his wily wordmongering ways. *Will Shakespeare could be a silver-tongued devil when he wanted something badly enough.* John laughed inwardly at the memory of his friend.

'… Another beer..?' Jack handed John a bottle of beer that had been cooling in a bucket of water from the river.

Jane fed Lilibet ready for bed before climbing into the waggon to go to sleep. The men chatted for a while longer, while Jack finished smoking his pipe. When he finally retired for the night John threw a few more logs of wood onto the fire to ward off any animals and set one or two aside for when they woke. Both men had seen to their respective horses earlier in the evening, but John couldn't help wandering over to Major, rubbing his muzzle for comfort. He spoke to him gently as he patted him. Thanking him for his companionship and sure-footedness.

'I don't know what I'd have done without you boy' said John, hugging him thankfully. 'Just one more obstacle to overcome now boy… You can do it 'we' can do it. We have to do it!' John looked up to the stars, closed his eyes. No words were necessary. *Whatever was in his heart would be heard if there's anyone listening*, he thought, and wrapped his blankets round him to settle down near the fire.

Chapter Twenty

He has to be in time

John woke up to the sound of the baby screaming. He'd been struggling to sleep all night, already worried that he was wasting time. His wife could be lying dead before he could even get home! Reluctantly, he had to admit Jack made sense, starting fresh the next morning in daylight. The waters of a tidal river could be treacherous during the day, let alone at night. It might have been the sensible thing to do, but it didn't stop John feeling guilty.

Now that he was awake, John was keen to get going. Jack was already checking on his horse, John joined him.

'I'll see to the horses' said Jack; 'if you could grab some kindling for the fire for Janey. She'll make us all breakfast before we set off once she's settled baby. I've already caught us some fish - I couldn't sleep, what with baby and all… Toss your blankets and saddlebags onto the waggon. No use weighing down the poor horse with wet blankets now is there? Keep 'em dry if we can – yes?' he gave a smile and a wink in John's direction and turned to continue checking and feeding the horses.

Janey's food was as satisfying as Jack said.
'My wife can make something out of nothing if she's a mind.' He said.

Crossing the river

John had crossed the river many-a-time before, but usually in a boat, with the horse swimming behind. Major was no stranger to swimming. Once over he would have had no problem swimming the river either, but it had been some time since he'd had to even try. *I hope I can still do it,* he thought *I'm not getting any younger.* He tried not to dwell on such matters.

'I've crossed this river before.' John told Jack. 'Usually in a boat, but if we cross at its shortest point while it's low tide, the water will be slack with very little movement. It's the middle distance that the horses might struggle. The river deepens and they'll have to swim. It's not too far, only some six hundred feet or so, I reckon, at its lowest. The horses should be able to walk much of the distance before the river deepens.'

'That's good to know' said Jack. 'We can work this together, I'm sure. Can I suggest we let the horses walk from here to the river, alongside one another, give them a chance to get used to each other's pacing, you ride your horse as they walk, to reassure him, me and Janey will ride on the waggon to guide our horse with the reins, just to begin with, then as we feel the riverbed fall away and the horses begin to swim, you and me both jump into the water, hold each of our horses and guide them to the other side 'til they regain their footing. How's that with you John?'
'Sounds like a plan to me, Jack,' winked John, glad to simply be on their way at last.

Jack had already noted the river's height when he was fishing. He'd crossed enough rivers in his time and knew exactly what he was looking for. There weren't many surprises he hadn't experienced in his many years of travelling and this was going to be nothing special, in-fact it was one of the shortest rivers he'd crossed. He felt pretty confident the crossing wouldn't cause a problem... as long everyone knew their part and the waggon didn't become unbalanced by anxious horses. Jack had only one concern and that was John. He was in so much of a hurry that Jack was worried the horses might pick up on his anxiety and become fractious. It was imperative that they remain calm and reassured by their drivers as they crossed. A silent prayer was released under Jack's breath as they set off.

They had only a short time before the ebbing low tide began to flow back to its full flow again, about half an hour of slack time. As it was, the horses had made good time swimming the deepest part of the river and were soon touching land again despite being under deepening waters. Both horses did their owners proud, and John, who had also been worrying about his companions, felt only glad to be still alive. He'd got cramp in one of his legs but had managed to keep going with the help of his now *trusty steed!* He was glad to feel land under foot by the end of it and the men guided the horses to firm ground, securing the now dripping wet waggon while Jane gathered kindle for a fire. They were all exhausted and the sooner they could dry off, and rest the sooner they could be on their way again.

John wasn't so sure about stopping. He was frustrated. He wasn't far away now; less than half a mile. Twenty or thirty minutes at most and he'd be home, but he felt obligated to his companions. They had a baby to consider and a waggon to dry out. So after ensuring everything was done - horses settled, firewood gathered, everything needed for camp, John told Jack he would walk on, *he had to be with his wife!* He knew his horse needed to rest and asked Jack for one more favour, to bring the horse to their home...

'I'll introduce you to everyone I know, and I know everyone,' grinned John. 'It'll be worth your while, I assure you,' he promised. Jack agreed, and looking over at his wife and daughter, he nodded and signalled to John to go - he understood.

After explaining his frustration to Jack and Janey, John set off as fast as he could. He'd given Jack directions to Hugh Gwynn's house and he and Ann lived nearby, they'd need only to ask anyone where John Punch lived, and they'd be shown the way.

A short walk along the trail and John's leg went into another spasm. His own fault, he should have had some fluids before setting off, his thoughtlessness cost him time. He tried to speed up. He was so close he could almost *feel* her nearness! The door was insight. There were people milling around, going in *and out of the house, his home...* John pushed past those who stood in the doorway and forced his way through the small group of people before they realized who it was pushing through. There were calls of 'John... John... John' as he rushed to his wife's side. He stopped short. The reverend was about to start some sort of ceremony. He placed a scarf of some kind around his neck and began muttering words. John wasn't listening. He stood silent. Looking at his wife; then he kneeled beside her and took her hand, touched her forehead, her hair. Not wanting to look at the reverend for fear of what he might see, he looked about for a face he recognized. Hugh came close, touching him on his shoulder and gently whispered in his ear

'She's nearing the end. I didn't know what else to do… please forgive me?'

'The medicine!' John yelled. His thoughts went straight to the medicine, the reason for his journey. He'd forgotten the bag!! How could he have been so stupid? Scrambling to his feet, he stood, held his wife's face in his hands and kissed her forehead. He had to find them. Jack and Jane; he had to find them. *They couldn't be too far behind him* he thought and started running back along the trail he'd only moments earlier ran along.

'Stupid… Stupid… Stupid! How could he have been so stupid!' he scolded himself as he ran. Almost at the point of exhaustion he heard horses and waggon wheels ahead of him. Thrusting his arms out, he screamed - 'STOP!'

Jack pulled the horse's reins to halt their movement. John ran straight to his horse frantically looking for his saddlebags, then realizing he'd packed them on the waggon before crossed the river, he ran to look in the back, grabbing at the sides for support as he made his way round. They weren't there!

'Where are my bags?' he yelled! 'I need my bags!' Jack was trying to get his attention to tell him that they were beside him after he'd noticed that they'd been left behind, but John was so crazed with worry… his hands flaying around in frustration, he wasn't looking. Jack jumped down from his seat, grabbed John's arms to get his attention, and showed him the bags. John snatched them from him and began running back home. Jack climbed onto the waggon, caught him up and told him to climb on-board.

'We'll get there quicker than you running John; you're exhausted. Now get on – NOW!' he ordered John firmly.

'I have to get the medicine to her!' said John, anxious, frantically climbing on to the rig. 'I saw her... She's serious...' John spoke between gasps. 'They're saying prayers...'

'Yahh!' Jack jerked the horse's reins to move them as quickly as he could, along the rough track of the little-used island trail. John held tightly onto his bags. To John the journey seemed to be taking ages, but in reality, they reached Gwynn's homestead in no time.

'Whoa' called Jack as they neared the housed area. John jumped off the waggon that had barely stopped and ran into his home, falling on his knees at his wife's bed side. Grappling in his bags, he plunged a hand inside to reach for the medicine. Something sharp penetrated his skin once, then twice, as he grabbed for the bottle. He threw the bag away and momentarily pulled his hand towards his mouth to ease the pain.

Turning back to his wife, he removed the lid... then he remembered something Perenelle had said – a few drops... in water. He turned to the priest 'Water... I need water.' John was waving his good hand around gesturing to be given water and something to pour it into. Hugh and the priest, almost in sync, placed a cup in his hand, and poured water from a bottle that the priest was holding. John poured a few drops into the water. Elizabeth raised Ann's head so as not to choke on the fluid being poured into her mouth. John eased Ann's lips apart and gently dribbled the potion between her lips encouraging her to swallow as best he could. Ann was weak, but for a moment she became responsive and began swallowing.

'A little more Ann… come on girl, you can do it, for me – John, come on… drink!' He pleaded with her. She began to choke, and cough, but swallowed. John stopped to look at her. *She was going to be all right – he knew it; she just had to be.* Then suddenly he collapsed.

The doctor, who had returned when he saw the waggon arrive, rushed to John's side.

'What happened?' he asked the room of people, looking around for someone to answer. There were shaking of the heads by some then someone called out

'He was fine until he put his hand in the bag.' The doctor looked carefully into the bag and saw the two-headed snake. He looked back at John.
'What have you been up to now, you silly man?' said the doctor shaking his head. He examined John's hands and found four holes where the snake's fangs had pierced his skin. The doctor had seen enough snake bite injuries to know that if they had fangs like those, they were likely to be venomous.

'Pass my bag' called the doctor. He carried all sorts of remedies with him, but after searching through his concoctions, the one thing he needed was missing – plantain! He'd not got round to replacing it…

'Hey, you!' the doctor pointed to a woman standing by the doorway. Go and pick some plantain. There is usually some amongst the uncut grasses. Boil it in water for about half an hour, then, fetch it to me. Quick woman quick!' he shot out his instructions and turned back to his patient. 'What on earth was he doing with a two-headed snake in his bag' muttered the doctor under his breath as he searched once more in his bag for an alternative solution.

Taking out his knife, he instructed Hugh and a concerned looking stranger standing by the door, to place John on the bed next to Ann. The elderly doctor struggled to his feet as they did so. He held the knife over a lit candle to sterilize it. The two men lifted John onto the bed as instructed while the doctor searched in his bag for another ingredient, this time he found what he was looking for and placed the bottle in his pocket. He looked around the room.

'If there are any ladies present who are a bit squeamish you may want to leave now, for what I have to do is not pleasant I'm afraid.' And he paused whilst Elizabeth and one or two others left the room.

Elizabeth had other reasons for wanting to leave the room. She had recognized 'the stranger' who had been standing at the door. It was her son, Jack. Had he seen her? Did he recognize her? She needed to leave the room if only to compose her own emotions which were now running out of control. She had never found the right time to tell Hugh about her son... his son – 'their' son. After all these years, what would Hugh say? What would he do? Would he still want her? Would he be angry? Would he want her out, or leave her, like her son had all those years ago! Her mind was filled with a myriad of questions all of which were dwarfed by a singular question – would they forgive her?

Her son had never given her a chance to explain. Hearing his grandfather calling him a *bastard son* had been a shock. He was young, but old enough to understand what the words meant. What hurt more than anything was the look on his face, that look haunted her to this day. The look of shock as he looked around the room at the faces of Elizabeth's family, followed by dismay and disillusionment as he looked in her direction... then came the look of anger and disgust... He'd stormed off into the night never to be seen or heard of again... until today. How was she going to face him? He was bound to have questions, and Hugh, her darling Hugh? Elizabeth didn't know what she was going to do. Walking back to the house she convinced herself that she hadn't been noticed and busied herself tidying her room then sat down darning Hugh's socks. A mindless chore and something she could do without thinking.

The doctor took hold of John's hand to examine the bites. He had to get the poison out as quickly as possible. He instructed Hugh to hold John's hand steady whilst he cut a straight line across the marks where the poison had entered. After squeezing some blood out of the wounds, he removed the bottle from his pocket and poured its contents over the cuts. Ammonia – the next best thing he had to hand to at least 'try' to counteract the poison.

'How about the medicine he just gave his wife, why not try that too?' suggested Hugh to the doctor.

'Indian medicine – poppycock!' retorted the reverend derisively.

'No, no,' said the doctor 'It has been well talked about that much of the medicines used by native Indians have been useful in curing many ailments. Hand me the bottle and give me some of that water you gave John earlier for his wife,' instructed the doctor. The reverend reluctantly did as he was told.

'Only a few drops he said, didn't he?' he asked Hugh for reassurance. Hugh nodded and passed the now empty bottle of holy water back to the reverend that the doctor had handed to him. 'Hold his head up man,' said the doctor irritably. The reverend lifted John's head to drink. A little of the liquid fell to the bed, but with a little coaxing the doctor managed to get quite a bit of the fluid past John's lips. 'There's nothing more we can do now but wait,' said the doctor.

'Everyone can go now, there's nothing more to see here – be off!'

Hugh, the reverend and the doctor, remained. Everyone else wandered off to go about their business.

'I'll just be outside' said Hugh, removing his pipe from his jacket and opening the door. *It could be a long wait the doctor had said. Where was Elizabeth?* He wondered.

Chapter Twenty One

United at last

After helping to lift John onto the bed, Jack could do nothing more for his new friend. He should be setting up camp for the night, he needed to be ready to sell his wares in the morning, but he found himself wandering aimlessly *'looking for a good site'*, or so he told his wife, but something had been niggling him.

The face of the woman who left the room when the doctor asked people to leave, she'd looked familiar, a little older and grey-haired, but... it couldn't be, could it? He stopped in his tracks as the realization suddenly hit him! He needed to find out. He needed to find her. He needed to be sure. Could it really be, after all these years - his mother? It had been a long time.

He started searching, his eyes seeking everywhere. People were hanging around outside John's home. He was about to give up when he turned round and saw her, sitting on the porch of the big house. Elizabeth looked up at just that moment. She saw her son staring over at her, a look of disbelief on his face. She rushed to enter the house. Fear, suddenly struck her! Unsure of his reaction, she wanted to run. To postpone any confrontation with him, for as long as she possibly could. *If she were inside the house she'd have a door between them.* Her heart was racing. Her breath quickened. Fear… or excitement, she wasn't sure. She wanted so much to run to him, to hold him. There was no oxygen in the air. Her head felt like it was going to burst with indecision. Jack called out to her as he ran to the house. Elizabeth was just about to walk through the door…

'MOTHER!' he yelled. Elizabeth halted, afraid to turn about. Like a rabbit caught in a trap every nerve in her body screamed RUN! Elizabeth couldn't move. She heard footsteps behind her halt, then the voice of her son again…

'Mother…' his voice was deep and calm, different to the last time she'd heard him. He spoke quietly, was that affection she'd heard? Elizabeth turned round to face him, and the emotion of the moment almost caught her breath as she saw her son's face smiling at her. His arms open wide. She could only stand and look at his worldly worn, face as he approached and hugged her. The tears that had never been wept came flooding through. There they stood for a long while…

Regrets – we all have them

Hugh felt totally helpless. Usually, he knew what was needed and would either do it himself or give orders for the task to be done, but seeing both his friends just lying there was tearing at his heart. John was his best friend. Over the years he had become his only true friend. In the world of politics, a world Hugh now lived in, there was no such thing as a true friend. His job took time and energy, with barely enough time for his family! There had been times when he needed a friend. Someone to whom he could unburden himself without being criticized or judged and John had been there for him.

In his younger days it had been his wife Ann-Joyce who would listen to him. It was one of the reasons he felt so responsible for her death. She had shared his worries, been his confidante, even after she became ill and her heart was weak, she'd still been his rock, strong and reliable. He'd continued to unburden himself to her, never considering the strain he was putting on her, she bore it all.

After she passed he had no one to confide in. He began drinking heavily, feeling sorry for himself, never a thought for his children. John helped him through all that, through his grief. It was John who helped him to take control of his life again. John had become his new confidante. He had been there for him all these years. He couldn't bear it if anything were to happen to him.

They'd become really close friends. He'd never been able to make up for that one time when he had misjudged him. Hugh remembered it as vividly as if it were yesterday.

It was the year he'd been given a share of the island on which they now lived. He'd saved a young Indian girl from drowning many years' earlier. When she grew up, and her father died, she wanted to show her gratitude to Hugh; she gave him land, an island. He automatically claimed it in the name of the King of England. A few years later, realising that he would have to honour the indentures that were nearing their end, he asked for a portion of the land to be used for that purpose, he was granted 1000 acres on the island, almost a whole island! He was thrilled, but had to sign the patent for the land at court. Upon his return he was told by his overseers that in his absence two of the servants were missing - *plus John!* They told him smugly.

Hugh had been travelling for days, he was weary. His plan had been to get the land, and give John his fifty acres in due course - it was to be a surprise... and he'd run away? Hugh was furious!

He had had it all planned out. They would still be able to work closely together. He would have the land, John would help him to divide it up to pay each indentured servant what they were due along with a year's supply of corn as agreed, and John... well John would have the pick of the best acres, plus he would guarantee Ann's land to be adjacent to John's when her time came too. Selfishly, he'd also hoped that John would continue working with him, it was going to be hard work, but they'd made a good team. The future was looking good. He'd have been set for life!

All his plans were for nought. How could John be so ungrateful? Wasn't he happy working on the plantation? Had he felt mistreated in any way? Why didn't he say if he wasn't very happy? A myriad of questions ran through Hugh's mind at once, but only one kept resounding - why did he betray his trust... he thought he was his friend?

John had always been trustworthy, reliable and loyal! But where the hell was he? He couldn't believe it, but what reason did the overseers have to lie? John would have told him if he was unhappy wouldn't he?

How could he do this to him, how could John betray his trust like this, after taking him into his trust, befriending him? John was a good man. Educated, sensible, good with people, he even spoke several languages. Men, women and children loved. Hugh's own children loved him – it didn't make sense for him to run away without saying anything.

Hugh's confusion had turned to anger and he had ordered the three men to be found and brought to him, he would avenge his own condign punishment upon them when they returned.

For a while Hugh had struggled to cope with all the workload that John had handled for so long. He berated himself for allowing himself to become so reliant on one person. He hadn't realized how reliant he had become on John. Since becoming a member of the House of Burgess, he'd given more and more responsibility to John and now... he needed to sort this out!

Weeks passed before he had heard anything more about the runaways. Then one day he received a summons to attend court, 9th July 1640. The men had all been caught and were awaiting sentencing. *They should have been returned to him,* he thought, *he'd been the one to send the sheriff's men to capture the runaways.* If the stories were true about Governor Calvert, John would be lucky to get away with his life! He had to speak to John and at least now he finally knew where to find him

His first act had been to see John. Find out what the hell he was doing, running away?

'I thought we were friends, John? I thought you could talk to me. Why?' demanded Hugh when he saw him. 'Why did you run away?' he'd yelled in frustration.

'I came looking for you. I wanted to your permission...' Hugh angrily, cut him short.

'Permission for what..?' Hugh had demanded, wondering what had been so important that John would take the risk of leaving the plantation without permission.

When he'd told Hugh about his plans and about the other servants running away and following him, Hugh suddenly felt guilty for being so mistrusting.

'It's all happening at once.' John explained, frustrated. He'd read about the new marriage laws. Clergymen were compelled to keep records of every marriage. Then a few months later there was to be a mass baptism by a missionary priest, baptizing an Indian Chief, Chief Kittamaquund, his wife and family, which gave John an idea of his own. Maybe he could take part in the ceremony? Then the best news of all was about a priest who had bought land on which he'd built a Manor and had land to lease to tenant farmers; people whose indentures were ending. With his and Ann's indentures soon to end, John wanted in on that too!

It was a lot for Hugh to take in. John wasn't running away *from* him, he was running *to* him, he wanted his blessing to be baptized and lease land and he needed Hugh's permission for them both. *How could it be that good intentions should end up being punished?* Thought Hugh!

'I didn't mean to cause all this trouble.' John apologized profusely. He could see Hugh shaking his head in disbelief, wondering what could he do?
'But why did you drag the other two with you?' Hugh had asked.

'I didn't.' replied John. 'They started to follow me. I couldn't shake them off. I couldn't persuade them go home' he explained. 'so I tied turning back towards the plantation thinking that they might follow me back, but they didn't. Then I heard a commotion in their direction and suddenly I was surrounded by men, grabbed and thrown into a cart, and ended up here! They wouldn't listen to me. I told them to send you a message. You're here, so I guess they must have told you?'

'I've been summoned to attend court, John – 9th July and to be honest I fear that it could be the death penalty for you. Governor Calvert hates and detests anyone who is not a Christian. He believes that everyone who does not believe in the Holy Trinity should be put to death. That's why I told them to bring you all back to me, but you ended up here! I'm not sure what I can do to help, but I'm going to try John… I'm going to try.
Hugh had felt terrible for not trusting John. All he'd ever wanted was to make his wife happy. John had told Hugh how Ann had never felt she was proper wife, not in the eyes of her God; her faith meant everything to her. She'd always seemed happy enough though. He remembered telling John he'd have to be baptized before her could be given the sacrament of marriage. He too, had heard about the missionary, Father White performing a baptism and marriage ceremony for Chief Kittamaquund, so

he knew what he was saying was true, but he hadn't given it much thought at the time. He had to see what he could do for John, before it was too late.

'Worst possible scenario,' he told John 'after death, is branding. The governor likes to make an example of runaways by marking them with the letter 'R' on their cheek. He's also fond of the lash. The court is likely to extend your indentures. I will write to the court, see what I can do.' He remembered telling him.

It was the end of May when he submitted a request to the court for leniency. He asked that they allow him to mete out his own condign punishment on his servants. They wrote back on 4th June telling him he had to put his own case before the Governor in writing and make a direct plea for leniency.

Hugh wrote to Governor Calvert that very day explaining there had been a misunderstanding. The men weren't runaways, they were meant to be going with him to see Father Copley about leasing farmland. He had explained how John was a good man, hardworking, honest, trustworthy, a good husband and family man, and loyal. He hoped that a little white lie wouldn't be questioned, after all, he was a member of the House of Burgess and a Justice of the Peace surely his position warranted some element of trust?

Unfortunately, Governor Leonard Calvert was well-known for his harsh sentencing of non-Christians. He considered himself a fair man. He believed that all baptisms in the name of Christ were equal, but it was God forbid anyone who was not a Christian. He had little tolerance for those of other faiths, but was willing to show leniency to them at least, but non-believers…

Hugh had pleaded for tolerance for John on the grounds that he was intending to be baptized by Father Copley, but Calvert refused to be persuaded. He asked once again, as the man suffering the loss, could he be granted permission to mete out his own condign punishment to his servants, for them to be sent back to him for punishment? But the Governor was intent on making an example of the men under his new law on Religious Tolerance that he and his family had been fighting for these past few years.

It was soon the 9th July. Governor Calvert, himself, was not in attendance, but he instructed the Assembly on his decision. He would return the three men to Hugh AFTER he and the court had meted out their own punishments.

The men James and Victor were ordered to be given thirty lashes a piece, as was John. James and Victor however were given one year each added to their indentures working for Hugh plus three years serving the colony by way of recompense, whilst John's indentures were extended for his whole life!

Hugh had been allowed two concessions, there would be no branding on any of them, Hugh could decide if he wished them to be branded, and the death penalty was removed for John, but in its place, John's indentures would be extended to life-long, to Hugh *'or his assignst'*.

A broken friendship

Although John was grateful to Hugh for saving his life, the 'concessions' Hugh spoke of meant very little to John. He had still lost his good name. His reputation was scarred for life, as was his back. John was especially unforgiving of Hugh's mistrust of him! John had always been proud of his reputation, in the knowledge that even if they didn't like him, they could respect him. It was all gone! Working with someone who didn't trust him… John could think of nothing that would ever mend their friendship.

Hugh - 1642 – Gwynn's Island

Two years had passed. The land that Hugh had requested and signed for, was finally given permission to be used *and about time* thought Hugh. He needed John more than ever. There would be much to do mapping out the island, sectioning it off. He'd need to choose his own prime location first. And they'd need more labourers. Labourers to replace the servants he was about to lose and labourers to clear the island for development. Specialist men to build houses, it would be all hands on deck from now on, and he still had his legal responsibilities and the plantation to consider.

'How many servants will be needed?' he spoke aloud to himself 'John will be able to work that out first thing.' Then Hugh stopped. He realised he was remembering how well he and John had worked together in the past. With tensions the way they were, he'd have to try to find some way of getting John back on track. He decided to sleep on it 'til morning.

As a soldier, Hugh had learnt to listen to his gut. If something wasn't going right don't try pushing forward until you have a plan. Military common sense he told himself. With that thought in mind, he went to sleep hoping that a solution would come to him. Genuine friends were hard to come by in this harsh new world. Winning back John's friendship was important. He decided to sleep on it.

The next morning Hugh set his plan into motion. John turned up at his usual time, ready to do his duty. Hugh ordered John to organise some strong men with the appropriate tools and load up the waggon with all that would be needed for the next few days. Around noon they were ready to leave. With a thousand acres of rich farmland to measure out and mark they had a lot of work to do and Hugh hoped to get everything done in one fell swoop. Most of the time was passed in silence between Hugh and John except for the minimum necessary communications. Then on their last night Hugh broke the silence to ask one important question about Ann's indentures.

'She has only one more year left before she is free of her indentures. Has she decided what she's going to do yet?' Hugh asked John. Hugh was aware of the predicament ahead of John and Ann. They were still a married couple, yet Ann would soon be free of her indenture, able to go anywhere she chose. She'd have her freedom dues – a few acres of land with a house and crop seed to get her farm started, but John was indentured to himself for life!

'We've not discussed it.' Was all John would say, moodily moving away so as not to be called upon to say more. Suddenly, Hugh realised how he could make amends and hopefully get his friend back. He just wasn't sure how John would feel about it.

John – the future must be face

John could see that Hugh was looking forward to living on such as lusciously rich and fertile island. He had chosen an ideal location for his family's new home. Close enough to the river to get fresh water, and good healthy soil. But Hugh had hit the nail right on the head when he asked about Ann's plans for the future. It had been a subject that neither he nor Ann had wanted to discuss, and it certainly wasn't something John intended discussing with 'his master'! He left Hugh's question hanging in the air, but he knew that when he got home he'd need to broach the subject with Ann. They couldn't bury their heads in the sand much longer. Decisions had to be made. Preparations to be faced, he was tied to Hugh for the rest of his life, but Ann and Junior… they would be free.

John's not the only one unhappy with Hugh

Hugh and his men had been working away for almost a week, they were all exhausted. Cook prepared a delicious meal and Hugh spoke animatedly to his wife over dinner telling her of his plans for their new home et cetera. Not so enthused, she listened attentively to what he had to say. She had just become accustomed to long periods of isolation on the plantation and now he was talking of taking her onto an island, further away from civilisation. Hugh was oblivious to his wife's mood, never asking, always assuming that she would be as happy as he was. *She would have to pin him down and have a serious talk to him, but not tonight, tonight she would just let him get the excitement out of his system and let him sleep on it. She'd talk to him in the morning. He had to be told how she felt about moving… the morning, yes, the morning would be fine*, she told herself.

After dinner Hugh went outside to smoke his pipe before bedtime. He wanted to still his mind before retiring for the night. His wife gave her final instructions to the servants before going up to bed and came to Hugh to kiss him goodnight. A kiss that was less passionate than he'd hoped. He knew then that something was bothering her. She was already in bed by the time he made his way upstairs. The night was warm so he opened the shutters to let in some air. A faint light from the night sky shone across his wife's face to show her eyes firmly closed and a slight frown between her eyes, she wasn't asleep. Climbing into bed he snuggled up to her hoping to work off some of the excess energy he felt, but she was having none of it, turning away from him to show disinterest. He snuggled up closer and raised her nightdress to get closer. She turned once more, this time to face him her eyes open, then closed as they met his. Hugh had been dismissed.

Hugh has a proposition

Frustrated and annoyed, Hugh dressed and went downstairs. His body was tired but his mind wouldn't let him rest. He decided to work on his map of the island, mapping out what he could from memory and marking out which piece of land was his. With at least a two-day ride between the island and the plantation there was no way he intended to do that every week, and he'd farm something different on the island, he didn't know what yet, but it would definitely not be tobacco. The island would be a new start, a new beginning for himself and his family.

Hugh finished what he could, but the subject of Ann, John's wife, still bugged him, the thought of breaking up a marriage because of John's life-long indentures and leaving his wife and son without a husband and father, but if everyone was agreeable he hoped he had the solution. They'd all worked well together until that unfortunate incident. He couldn't let it go on indefinitely, something had to break. John was a proud man and Hugh had failed to trust his loyalty, it was understandable that he felt betrayed, John was now his prisoner!

Unable to rest he decided to speak with them both. John answered the door sullenly, none too pleased at being interrupted at such a late hour.

'I need to speak with Ann...' announced Hugh, John didn't move, just looked blankly at the unwelcome visitor. The door opened wide revealing a sombre Ann.

'Ann, I need to ask you something, may I come in?' Ann stepped back to allow their visitor to enter. 'May I sit?' Hugh didn't wait for an answer and sat in one of the chairs nearest the fire uninvited, Ann's chair. Ann took a seat at the table nearby.

'I apologize for the lateness, but this can't wait any longer.' Hugh looked from one to the other 'This tension between you and I John, has become untenable. You have every right to feel betrayed, and angry about the sentencing, I accept that, but I have a proposition to put to you, to you both that is, that hopefully will put us back on an even keel.'

'Is this going to take long?' John asked curtly.

'Would you like some tea sir?' interrupted Ann remembering her manners. 'Errmmm er, hopefully not too long. Yes, dear lady, that would be most welcome.' Hugh was silent for a moment or two before he began speaking again and Ann had reclaimed her seat at the table.

'It's most important that the two of you hear me out before making any decision.' Both John and Ann looked at one another and nodded their assent.

'Your indentures will have reached their full term next year, Ann, have you given any thought as to how you're going to manage the land that you'll be entitled to, fifty acres of prime land on the island we've just returned from, and it's good land isn't it John?' Hugh didn't wait for a reply he wanted them to hear him out before they kicked him out. He continued with only a glance at his hosts' faces. Ann handed Hugh a cup of tea, which he graciously took and placed on the table that Ann had been sitting at. John took his and continued staring into the fire, not really wanting to listen to the conversation.

'Ahmmm, hmm…' Hugh cleared his throat, and took a quick sip of his tea before replacing it back onto the table, clearing his throat once again, he continued speaking, aiming his conversation at Ann. 'I have a proposition to put to you Ann… well, to you both. I've given this a great deal of thought and I hope it is agreeable to you.'

John's eyes looked over suspiciously at Hugh as he spoke, before returning to stare once again at the fire.

Noticing John's indifference, Hugh turned back towards Ann, his arms outstretched to indicate he needed specifically for her to listen.

'As I said when I arrived, your indentures will be ending soon, have you thought about what you're going to do with your land, or how you're going to manage?' Ann looked at John and shook her head. Neither of them had dared to look that far ahead. John would be tied to Hugh with his indentures, he'd have food and a roof over his head for the rest of his life, but she and Junior… they'd have their freedom dues, but what use is that if she has no one to share them with, Ann hadn't wanted to think about the future.

'Well I have,' Hugh told her firmly and I'd like to make you a proposition, to you both, this affects you too John. Please?' John didn't want to acknowledge the man's presence. They had been friends, but the trust had been lost when he received thirty lashes. He'd told himself he'd work with the man, but he didn't have to like him anymore. Hugh… the one person who he had come to respect and to trust, who he'd given his full allegiance to for all those years, the man who had become his friend; yet he didn't reciprocate that trust. Hugh waited for John to answer eventually he looked round at his wife and sat quietly facing Hugh.

'Well?' he asked

'As you both know John was faced with being branded with the letter 'R' on his face as a runaway or if the governor decided to make an example, John could have faced death for not being a Christian and having no faith at all! Did you realise that, did John tell you how serious it could have been?' John hadn't told Ann, she sat shocked by the news, but the look she gave him told him she'd deal with him later. After noting Ann's reaction, Hugh continued to speak 'John told me why he left the plantation. I spoke to directly with the governor rather than send him a letter as the assembly had advised. He wasn't easy to convince, and he wasn't prepared to be told how to run his court. On the day of the sentencing, I wasn't sure which way it was going to go, I'll be honest, but the sentencing John was given really was the best I could get for him under the circumstances. I am truly sorry that the sheriff's were sent to find him. They were supposed to bring them all back to me to be punished, not taken to Maryland!'

'You call thirty lashes and your prisoner - your slave, for the rest of my life, the best you could do?!' John stood up shouting with rage! Now my wife and I are looking at being separated because of it. She and Junior won't be able to manage the farm without me... what are they supposed to do now?' yelled John with frustration.

'John... John... calm down, take a seat, that's why I here – please... sit.' Hugh had stood up to face John and take control of the situation again. Ann looked still in a state of shock at the revelation, almost on the edge of tears.

'I miss our friendship John. I want to help. I think I have a solution, but I need you both to agree to it.' Hugh paused 'I've read and re-read the sentence of the court and they've given you life-long indentures with myself *'and my assigns'*! Now... I was also told I could not *'dispose'* of your indentures. I can't sell them on to anyone else they belong to me and me alone, but the law can be ambiguous at you know John, it's written like that deliberately, to leave it open to interpretation by cases that follow. I want to

'assign' you to continue helping me with my work as before...' John was about to interrupt, Ann signalled for him to remain calm and listen 'AND help Ann with her land, to live nearby our own home on the island and hopefully... be friends again?'
John just looked at Ann and Ann looked at John, neither could believe what they were hearing. Could it be as simple as that?

'Well, I'll leave that idea with you and take my leave for the night. See you in the morning John?' He looked at John, whose expression gave nothing away, and turned to Ann 'Thank you for the cup of tea, it was most welcome dear lady, goodnight.'

As the door closed behind Hugh, Ann locked it behind him and leaned against the door as she looked over at her husbands' bemused face. John raised welcoming arms to his wife and she crossed the room smiling with relief and hugged her husband tightly. A great weight had been lifted. Their future was looking good again. Then Ann burst out laughing. John looked at her as if she'd gone crazy.

'What's so funny?' asked John, not quite seeing anything to laugh about.

'Don't you see it John? For years you've said *I have your life*, I keep you busy running around after me so much that *you're like my slave* and now...' she laughed 'Now I own you! You're mine 'til your dying day!' she smiled fondly at her husband.' John, smiling in return

'So... *master*... what would you have me do?' teased John hugging his wife.

'There is only one thing I have to say to you right now and that is – take me!' She smiled a flirtatiously tantalizing, smile as John scooped her up in his arms, giggling like a young child.

Hugh faces his past

Hugh had left Ann and John to consider his proposition, he strongly believed they'd be happy to accept his offer, but right now, he had more important things to deal with. His wife had pushed him away and he needed to put his own house in order before he could move on himself.

It was late by the time he returned home. Ann's snoring told him she was already in a deep, undisturbable slumber. He lay alongside her and cuddled in to get warm apart from a momentary groan as his cold body touched hers, she barely acknowledged his presence. The day had been long and emotionally draining and soon Hugh fell into a fitful sleep waking the next morning unable to move. His arms… his legs… both tied tight!

He panicked for a moment between sleep and awake. He'd been dreaming he was captured, by people unknown, and hog-tied, but as he opened his eyes he realised he was in his own bed, still unable to move. The initial panic continued until he woke up fully to discover he was so tightly wrapped up in his bed sheets that he was cocooned like a caterpillar! Laughing at the foolishness of his situation he took a few moments to work out what to do. In the end his wife walked in to wake him and found him lying there and couldn't help but laugh at the sight before her. She decided to use it to her advantage.

At last she had her husband's full attention, he had no escape, he'd have to listen to her. She began explaining how she felt about his new project; she didn't want to move to a remote island no matter how lovely he described it. She'd just got used to living their lives on the plantation, she'd made some friends she could travel to within a day and back, and she'd made their house, a home. She needed Hugh to understand. She needed him to listen. Hugh lay in silence while she spoke. Not knowing how to respond. His silence only made Ann more sullen. She helped unravel the sheet in silence and walked away.

Hugh was relieved to be free. He'd once been captured when he was in the army and was reminded of his fear of losing control. Listening to his wife, but unable to move had brought it all back for a moment. It was stupid, but even though he knew, here and now, that he was safe, that he'd wrapped himself up so tightly that he couldn't move, he couldn't let go of the feelings of that time. Hugh washed hoping the cold water would wash away the feelings he'd thought were behind him. He dressed in silence. The joy of the previous day overtaken by his past memories, a past he'd never spoken about or admitted - to anyone.

Hugh – decisions, decisions

The next few days were a blur of activity. John and Ann accepted his proposal as Hugh had expected. Their friendship was still a little tense, but they were working on it. But he still had to find a solution that would please his wife. He *had* been listening throughout the flashback of emotion, but needed time to think of a solution that would satisfy them both. It would take time, but he'd found a solution to save his friendship with John, he was sure he would find something equally agreeable to please his wife.

It was something John asked him a few weeks later that prompted a solution. He asked the same question to Hugh as Hugh had asked of Ann. Have you thought about the future?

Both he and John had been so busy dealing with the new arrivals and allocating accommodation and food and shelter for the new servants that Hugh had left his wife to manage the plantation all on her own... She'd been managing well enough and if she was agreeable it could be the answer to both their problems.

Initially, Hugh was needed to oversee the island project *it was going to be the community he'd always dreamed of.* John could take over the project once the House of Burgess re-opened for the autumn sessions and Ann-Joyce could run the plantation which she loved, and it was a job she enjoyed. *Their house on the island that he'd spoke about could be their retirement home when they were older* he told himself.

That night he told Ann-Joyce of his suggestion. At first she was suspicious of his motives. She knew her husband liked to be in control of things and wondered why he was willing to relinquish his control over the plantation? Did he have another woman she asked him?

'Don't be silly woman! Where do I have time for another woman', he laughed, pulling her to him and giving her a kiss. It was the first time in a long time that she'd returned his affection, but soon their kisses became unexpectedly more amorous. Hugh wasn't going to question the change of attitude from his wife. He just longed to be touched in that special way. Hugh was breathless with passion as he whisked her up into his arms and carried her to their room. He wanted privacy for what was about to follow. Ann-Joyce was surprisingly ardent with her kisses which roused Hugh's affections even more. It wasn't long before they were both spent and lying breathless on the bed.

Ann-Joyce really was beautiful when she was womanly thought Hugh leaning over to kiss her gently, his arm over her upper body to hold her close. Their moments of closeness was so rare, he didn't want it to end too quickly. Together they fell asleep, both smiling in their glow of passion.

Chapter Twenty Two

A secret revealed

Finishing his pipe, Hugh knocked the funnel on the sole of his boot and set it on the window ledge of John's hut, to cool. Turning to go back into the hut, he glanced over at his home, the porch light was still on and it caught his eye. When he looked over, he froze in his tracks. His wife was hugging a strange man - in public, for the whole of the islanders to see! She was opening the door. She was inviting him into their home! For the briefest of moments Hugh was torn between his friend and his wife, but the decision was not difficult, he had to know who this man was, who so brazenly held his wife so closely! With all the emotion of the day looking for an escape, it didn't take long for the rage to grow inside Hugh. His pace speeded into a run.

At the same time as Hugh noticed his wife's shenanigans, another stood staring. A woman with a child was witnessing the same scene; it was Jane holding her baby. She had been wondering where Jack had got to. She and baby Lilibet had been waiting at the waggon after he told her he was looking for a suitable place to set up for the night. She was exhausted. Baby was restless... she was furious!

'I'll give him a place to set up for the night when I get hold of him' muttered the normally mild-mannered young woman now heading towards the house.

Hugh arrived moments before her and threw open the door! Entering his home, he saw the two of them about to sit down on the sofa near the fire looking all very familiar with one another. Elizabeth and Jack were startled as the door crashed open and Hugh rushed in. Then Jack saw his wife standing in the doorway and smiled, reaching out his hand to her.

Just at that moment, Hugh saw what he took to be an insulting smirk on the stranger's face. His fist clenched tightly, Hugh struck him hard!

'NO!' screamed Elizabeth, 'Let go of the boy!'

The young woman at the door gasped and held her baby closer to her. Hugh went to strike the stranger again, holding him down at the shoulder he raised his fist to strike a second blow...

'NOOOO!' Came a second scream from Elizabeth, grabbing her husbands' arm... 'He's your son!'

Hugh stopped mid-strike; his fist well-placed and ready to make its next blow count. He froze as his wife's words struck home. *His son...?* Hugh's mind became of whirl of questions, but none of them would form to speak. He looked at his wife; then at his son... shock, surprise, disbelief all flashing across his face at once. Elizabeth stood staring at her husband. Glancing occasionally at her son and the strange woman and child at her door; fear and anguish filled her thoughts, her whole body engulfed with apprehension. She could just reach back against the wall for support as she saw her husband rush out into the night.

Jack was mopping his bleeding brow as his wife took in the scene and moved closer, her eyes searching for answers.

'Jane…' he said, taking his wife by the shoulders and turning her to face Elizabeth, 'This is my mother.' Jack beamed at his family meeting for the first time. Elizabeth approached her daughter-in-law slowly, unsure what her reaction would be. What had Jack told her about his mother? Holding out her hand in greeting, the young woman moved closer and hugged Elizabeth - smiling. The child was between them,

'May I?' asked Elizabeth of its mother; gently moving the swaddling to see the baby's face.

'She's called Lilibet… After you…' Jane informed her, a look of pleasure on her face at finally meeting the woman her husband had often spoke about. Jack joined the trio, placing his arms about his two favourite women. They all took a moment to embrace, but then Jack's practicality kicked in.

'Well, I hate to spoil the moment, but we have to go and set up camp. It will soon be tomorrow, and Lilibet doesn't give us much time for sleep at night. Will you be all right mother? What about…'

'Your father..? He'll be all right.'

'And you?' Jack repeated.

'I'll be fine. I'm sorry I can't offer you a bed for the night. Not tonight at least, but maybe tomorrow? After your father has had time to calm down and I've had time to explain? Don't you two worry about me, good night.' They kissed and hugged and took their leave.

Meanwhile, Hugh's mind was racing. He was shocked at the news that he had another son! How? Why? When? All stupid questions; of course, he knew how and when, but they'd only spent that one night together? Why hadn't she told him? That explained why the old man hit him that time.

Ann, his wife, had finally arrived on the plantation with their eldest son John when Elizabeth turned up with a man much older than herself. In hindsight, he should have guessed he was her father. Elizabeth had not been able to stop her father from punching Hugh, but she did manage to drag him away, with a struggle. Hugh had not chased after them. His wife and child were watching. He let them walk away with no further explanation. His wife of course had been curious as to why he'd been hit, and Hugh had said something about his being a disgruntled workman and left it at that. It didn't make sense. Why had Elizabeth not told him? Why not say anything when they married, at least? All these years… she'd never given him any indication that they'd had a son together! Hugh's mind was awash with questions for her, but movement seen by the lamplight inside John's home made him wonder what was going on.

Where there's life there's hope

Hugh had barely walked through the door before he saw the doctor excitedly examining Ann. She was showing signs of recovery!

Reverend John was praying; prayers of thanks from the sound of them. Hugh looked hopefully at the scene inside, hopeful for the first time in a long time. He could hear Ann asking for water, but from John – there was still no sound, no movement.

'It's early days' the doctor pointed out reassuring Hugh when he noticed his worried face. 'The poison needs time to leave the body. I believe I cut most of it out, but it takes time. Don't you worry; could someone fetch refreshments, fresh water perhaps, for Ann?' he asked.

'Of course, of course' mumbled Hugh, looking round for Alice. 'I'll get someone' he said looking round outside. Alice appeared. She'd seen movement and was curious to find out what was happening, to be able to report back to Elizabeth.

'Ah Alice, just in time... Tell the mistress Ann is waking up and asking for water. Make sure it's been boiled.' He instructed.

Hugh's thoughts were all over the place. *How did he feel about the son he never knew he had? He wasn't sure. He was born from the love he had for his mother,* now his wife, he reasoned. *And he did love her with all his heart and body. The Elizabeth he first met was young and strong-willed. No one could force her to do anything she didn't want, not even marry the old man that her parents wanted her to marry. Marriage would have given her substance and security for sure, but Elizabeth... she wanted love, she wanted to travel, she wanted life! And that's what he loved about her... back then.*

He suddenly felt guilty. If it hadn't have been for him, she wouldn't have been trapped. She wouldn't have had to bring up a child on her own. Her parents, she'd told him already, had made her a 'companion' to her aunt. Elizabeth had told him that it was because she'd refused to marry the man, they chose for her. She obviously omitted to tell him she'd been outcast because of the child! *Why didn't she come to him,* he asked himself? No sooner had he thought it when he realized that was probably the reason for her visit with her father. She must have intended to tell him about his child, but seeing Ann at the door, carrying their son... that must have been what made her walk away. Hugh was going back and forth in his thoughts. Why... why... why? Always, he came back to the same thought – *she was ashamed. It was 'he' who was at fault. HE was the married one, not Elizabeth. It was HE who condemned her to live the life she did.* His heart was filled with remorse. Hugh returned to see his friends. Ann was looking at the doctor and saw he was examining John who was still unconscious. She reached out to John when suddenly there was a knock at the door. Hugh answered and there stood Elizabeth with a tray in hand containing soup, bread and freshly cooled boiled water. He opened the door wider to allow for the tray, taking a momentary glance in Hugh's direction, and then at Ann. *The tension was almost tangible.* Elizabeth had gone straight back into her nursing mode. She carried the tray to Ann's side and knelt down, placing the tray on the floor beside her. Ann had become agitated not knowing what was wrong with her husband. The doctor was busy with his patient and Elizabeth tried to explain what had happened. Hugh approached the bed hoping that his reassurance would help, but it just irritated Elizabeth who gave him a look that told him he was not needed. Hugh stepped back and took a seat and watched the ongoing scene before him. Elizabeth was trying to calm Ann down and gently tempt her with some nourishment, but Ann, being anxious about her husband, refused. Elizabeth became more assertive, insisting that she take at least a 'little' broth and a few sips of water, and with the renewed confidence that came from knowing her role as nurse as well as she did, Ann obeyed.

Hugh's eyes were watching his wife, she seemed different somehow, *or had he never really noticed her strength*? If only he knew what she was thinking? Hugh stayed quiet. In private he had never been a man of many words and at that moment he wasn't sure what to say and silence made a fool out of no-one.

The doctor had been busy all day, popping in and out, seeing to other patients. He needed rest and Reverend John was almost asleep on his feet.

'Go to ours,' Elizabeth told them both 'I've arranged for broth to be left next to the kettle near the fire in the kitchen, help yourselves. Cook will have retired for the night but she will have left dishes out for you, she was also fetching down some bedding for you both. The sofas in the main room should still get heat from the fire. Go and get some sleep... both of you. Hugh and I will stay with Ann and John.' She looked over at Hugh... he nodded agreement, awaiting his instructions of which there were none.

Only silence filled the room for a long time after Ann had drifted off into a more peaceful sleep, holding John's hand. After a while there was some small talk about their patients, then silence again. Neither one of them knew how to start the very difficult conversation that hung in the air between them.

It was almost dawn, Hugh was about to nod off, when Elizabeth finally broke the ice.

'I'm sorry.' That was all she could say. Tears she'd been holding back for years started pouring freely down her cheeks unheeded. Hugh reached out and held her while she wept. There was nothing he could say to ease her tears. What could he say? Nothing could wind back the years or change what had happened! He guided her back to the warm seat he'd been sitting on and sat next to her, his arms around her to keep her warm. She rested her head on his shoulder and just cried and sobbed, he hushed her trying to comfort her, but so much agonizing had been felt by Elizabeth, so many tears she'd had to control and now... it was like she'd never stop.

For Elizabeth it was like a great weight had been lifted from her. The tears flowed 'til they could flow no more, and exhausted, she fell asleep... in her lovers' arms. Jack, their son, was all she'd had left by way of remembering him for such a long time, the thought of losing Hugh again was unbearable. She'd never dared take the chance of telling him about Jack. She dreaded seeing the same look on Hugh's face that she'd last seen on her son's... Shock! Disbelief! Disillusionment and, was it anger? All she knew was that she'd lost her son she couldn't lose Hugh as well. So many times she'd tried to tell him, but her fear always stopped her. The longer she put it off the harder it got to say anything – until today. Fate – you can't cheat fate. It will not be denied.

Chapter Twenty Three

The sound of horses outside woke up the sleeping couple. Elizabeth's first instinct was to check that her patients were all right. Hugh's was to see what was going on. It was John's son with his wife and child. They'd been travelling for days and were all apologies for not arriving any sooner, but the river had slowed them down. He knew his mother was ill, but not his father. Hugh tried to tell them what happened, but John's son rushed past him. Ann was just rousing. Elizabeth stepped aside to let her son be near her.

'Your father has still not roused.' Elizabeth interrupted Junior's as he fussed over his mother. 'The doctor says, it's early days, and we're not to worry.' She wasn't sure how much he was listening to her, but his wife smiled and went to sit near John. Elizabeth nodded and smiled back, not a word was spoken. Suddenly Elizabeth felt in the way. Glancing at Hugh and pointing towards the door, they left:

'Hugh and I will go and rustle up some food for you all, leave you alone for a while, will you be OK?' She looked at Junior's wife as she grabbed Hugh's arm to leave. 'Your mother will be hungry. We shan't be long.'

Elizabeth and Hugh made their way home, away from the tiny hut. The whole household had heard the arrival of Junior's waggon as were rousing. Cook was already in the kitchen preparing breakfast while Alice set a new fire to heat water. Everything in the kitchen was in hand. Elizabeth wandered into the main room; Hugh was adding fresh logs to the dying embers in the fire place whilst being bombarded by questions from their guests. What was the noise all about and what was the status of their patients?

Hugh and Elizabeth were both glad to have their guests around as distractions. The prospect of being alone to discuss the previous evening's conversation was daunting. To their chagrin, they weren't saved for long. Their guests were hungry and keen to freshen up before breakfast, leaving their hosts alone in awkward silence.

Hugh finished 'safely' stacking logs on the fire, before picking up his pipe and inspecting it. Slowly tap, tap, tapping, he emptied the pipe over the fire then made a fuss about searching for his tobacco, which was, as he should have known, in its usual place on the mantel. He began filling it. Elizabeth had been watching as she folded the bedding ready to be put away, when...

'We have to talk.' They both spoke at the same time. They smiled and laughed at their synchronicity.

'After you' said Elizabeth,

'No after you' Hugh countered. Elizabeth cleared her throat and sat down. Pausing, she looked at Hugh, almost like an order, and waited for him to sit also. *This was going to be hard enough without him standing over her* she thought. As Hugh sat down opposite her, she nervously stood up, ringing her hands and searching for the right words. In the end, looking round the room, servants were going about their business. 'Let's go for a walk.' She suggested heading for the door and grabbing a shawl from the back of a chair as she did so. Hugh followed, not quite sure what to expect. As he exited the house, he carefully, deliberately, slowly shut the door behind him. He lit his pipe, watching as Elizabeth walked ahead, equally slowly; building up the courage, looking for inspiration about what to say next.

Hugh walked a little more briskly to catch up with her and stepped into pace beside her. Taking her hand by way of showing her that all was well with him, they walked silently together. Elizabeth didn't realize, but she'd been walking in the direction of their sons' waggon. She was still struggling for words when fate stepped in again; Jack, carrying freshly caught fish for breakfast, saw them just as he was returning. He smiled at his mother and looked at the man standing by her side…

'Hugh – I'd like to introduce you to your son!' she smiled at them both nervously, unsure of what more to say. Now it was up to the two men. There was an awkward pause, before Hugh made the first move.

'Son…' and he thrust out his hand in mock bravado, to shake. Jack reciprocated; then Hugh, unsure what he should do next, pulled his son closer, giving him a one-armed hug; Jack followed, and father and son were hugging 'awkwardly' for the first time, smiling and laughing nervously. Elizabeth could only return their smiles and give a silent thanks to whoever was listening, that they had accepted one another so readily.

Elizabeth had worried for years about this moment, yet as they began chatting, in this one wonderful moment in time, the two most important men in her life, were behaving as though they had known one another all their lives! She couldn't have asked for a better meeting of father and son.

She stood taking in the scene with relish. Hugh reached out to her. All three hugged. They were going to be all right. Her daughter-in-law... *their* daughter-in-law, and granddaughter, came over to see what was going on and for a few glorious minutes it was one big hug, until Elizabeth spoke again, laughing and smiling, and a little embarrassed.

'Well this is all well and good, and I don't want it to stop, but there's a young girl here who's getting hungry.' She looked at baby with that remark, 'Jack - bring those fish up to the house; Jane can have a break, cook will prepare them for your breakfast. I think it's time we all got to know one another properly.' She looked over at Hugh. Her confidence now back. Hugh couldn't have been happier. Seeing his wife becoming herself again, the woman he fell in love with was just wonderful. Giving his new daughter-in-law and granddaughter a hug, he carried the little one up to the house, talking to her all the way.

'You do realize she's only a baby Hugh', said Elizabeth with a smile that wouldn't leave her face. 'I know, I know, Grandmamma.' He said amused, continuing to ignore her.

Chapter Twenty Four

Ann was thrilled to see her son and his family. She'd not seen them since her grandson's christening. Excited as she was to see them, her mind was still pre-occupied with the information the reverend had given her the night before. She was struggling to give them the attention she'd have liked, but hoped they didn't notice.

The reverend had told her what John had done for her; how he had travelled north to seek help from a medicine woman and brought back a potion that she'd given him; a potion that made it possible for her to be alive; *but at what cost,* Ann wondered, looking at her husband lying pale-faced and drawn. She noticed how old he was looking. Despite being ten years her senior, John had never seemed old to her. He was as fit and healthy as any of the young men on the island. Always full of energy and enthusiasm, but he looked so old… so frail. She took hold of John's hand and fought back the tears that threatened to breach her composure. Listening to her guests proudly relating their stories about their son made her smile. She squeezed her husband's hand by way of acknowledging his presence as they spoke of his antics, or laughed. She knew her son was only chattering nervously because he didn't know how to respond any other way to seeing how ill his father was. He and his wife both tried to cheer Ann up and Ann was grateful for their cheeriness, but she hadn't been awake for long and she was beginning to feel weary. Alice arrived just in time, with a tray of food for them all and told her Reverend John was asking after her, and was waiting outside for news of how she was feeling this morning? Ann said to invite him in, to eat with them if he so wished. *His presence would take some of the pressure of herself trying to entertain her family,* she thought. She dearly loved them, and she'd missed them so much when they were so far away, but her immediate priority was with John... she wanted to just sit quietly and hold his hand... Willing life back into his still, lifeless body with all her heart! She was thankful to Reverend John at that moment; he was a welcome distraction for them all. He was just what the doctor would have ordered at that moment.

Reverend John had always had a soft spot for her husband. Hugh's son was in his teens when his mother died. He'd seen his father's anger at her death, how much he blamed God for taking her and he was feeling lost. Unable to talk to his father he turned to John, and herself. Between them they helped him to grieve for his loss. *Ann liked to think that she and John had, in some small way, helped the reverend to become the man he was today. Her faith had always been important to her and John's kindness...* she smiled as she remembered, and laid a hand on John's body to feel closer to him. John was not a believer in God, any God for that matter, but he lived, what the reverend would call 'a god-fearing life, a Christian life' - good and kind. He loved Ann so much that he would even join her in prayer *(if he couldn't find anything else to do), just to make her happy.* She laughed a little inside, remembering how he would seek out any job he could so as not to be available to pray with her!

'If your God is everywhere like you say he is, he doesn't need me to sit and pray with you to hear me. Every morning I give thanks for simply being alive! I thank the sun for rising, the winds and rain for watering the plants and you, my lovely wife, for fixing my food, for caring for me. What more could you ask of a working man like myself?' he'd announce holding his hand to his heart and giving her his cheeky smile and a wink.

She and John had spent so many hours with Hugh's son. Some days he would talk about his mother, others he would simply chatter about his day. He seemed to find comfort and strength just being around them. She felt proud of what he'd achieved and was comforted by his presence.

'The mistress told me to tell you that you and your guests are welcome to join them later in the big house, if you're up to it?'

'Thank you Alice,' Ann replied, 'but I need to sit with John, I need to be here when he wakens, but Junior..? Maybe you would like to visit them later?' Ann suggested hopefully, as Alice left.

Alice had placed the tray of food on the table for everyone to help themselves and added logs to the fire before leaving. They all sat round the table to eat. Mary, Ann's daughter-in-law, was occupied feeding the little one, while the two men talked quietly together and Ann closed her eyes to rest a-while, her breathing synchronising with her husbands, it made her feel closer.

She must have been so tired that she'd fallen asleep, for the next she knew was waking up lying on the bed. She reached out her hand for John – he wasn't there!

Sitting up sharply, the room was dark and empty. Firelight revealed a plate of food left on the table. A smell of coffee hung in the air from a pot placed near the fire on the hearth. John… where was he? Ann began to panic! She grabbed for the lamp next to the food and knocked the plate of food onto the floor with a clatter. As she bent down to pick it up, the door opened and in walked John!

He rushed to Ann's side and knelt beside her grabbing her hands in his and kissing them. She touched his bent head and reached for his chin. She wanted only to look upon his face, so full of concern, filled with joy at seeing her awake again. As they faced each other John pulled her to her feet, squeezing her tightly -

'I can't breathe John' she laughed, looking into her husband's face with such tenderness. She loved this man so much her heart felt like it would burst with happiness!

People started appearing all around as news spread to their families that Ann was awake. There was excitement in the air that Ann couldn't quite understand, *she'd only been asleep a few moments hadn't she,* she thought?

'Ann,' John's excitement couldn't be contained any longer, 'Ann,' he repeated, taking both her hands in his once again and getting down on one knee. Ann laughed

'What are you doing old man?' she chuckled looking 'round at the slowly filling room. Her son and his family entered; Hugh and Elizabeth came in close behind.

'Stop messing about John, you're embarrassing me.' Ann wriggled with embarrassment.

'Ann...' John's face took on a more serious look and he held her hands firmly in his, forcing her gently to face him. 'We've been together for a long time. You have been my strength, my love, the mother of our child' John turned his head to look at his son; 'You have been my wife and taken on my name, but in name only have we been wed, and that has been down to our good friends Hugh and Elizabeth...' he once again looked round to acknowledge them both with his playful wink.

'John, come on... stop it, you're going to hurt yourself kneeling down like that.' Ann pulled on her husband's hands to get him to stand up – he did - with a struggle. They both laughed as he composed himself once more and stood straight before her.

'Ann.' John was done laughing 'Reverend John is only here for a few more days. He's agreed... and this really depends if you still want to... he's agreed to marry us. We'll be married in the eyes of your God; well our God really, or should I say... Oh Ann... will you do me the honour of agreeing to marry me - again?' Seeing a blank expression on Ann's face, John was beginning to worry that it was too little too late. He began explaining.

'I've discussed it with the reverend and he has agreed to baptize me.'

'I'm so sorry it didn't happen sooner' interrupted Hugh, feeling guilty about the last time John had tried to be baptized.

'No, no Hugh' said John, silencing his friend, 'that was a long time ago, and today is the first day of the rest of our lives.' Looking back at Ann. 'It is the future that I want us to look at now, Ann...' he repeated 'Will you marry me?'

Ann still stood looking at her husband in surprise! She couldn't believe her ears. *Was she dreaming,* she wondered? Finally, with all eyes upon her, she replied...

Yes... oh yes, John - yes!' Beaming happily; they kissed and hugged, not caring who was watching! *At last she would be a real wife no longer bearing the guilt of living in mortal sin.* The crowd whooped and cheered eventually dispersing only after Hugh sent them all away. *His friends needed to be alone.*

There's a wedding to plan

The next couple of days were a whirl of excitement. The whole island was alive with busy-ness. John was intent on making it a day to remember, to give his wife the wedding she'd always wanted, the wedding she deserved and all those who had any time to spare, was set to work by Hugh. There was a lot to do and finally Hugh felt he could be useful.

When John had first woken after being poisoned, seeing Ann beside him so still, he'd thought he'd lost her. His heart missed a beat until he was told she was merely asleep! The relief! She'd slept for two whole days! John had stood vigil the whole time only leaving her bedside to eat. Reverend John kept him company when others were coming and going. It did give John time to speak with him on a private matter he'd never discussed with anyone else.

John related the whole story to him, the treacherous journey, the scary moments and the desperation he felt. He confided in him about the many prayers he'd spoken during those exhausting days, the promises he'd made… He was embarrassed to ask, but he was also genuine. He wanted only to know how he could keep his promises?

'If what you have told me John, is true, if you are now a true believer and if you're prepared to follow the path of the Lord, I see no reason why you should not be baptized. You'd have no further reason not to be able to marry Ann', he laughed. 'In fact, if you will permit me, I would be honoured to be the one to carry out both ceremonies, that's of course, if you will let me?' he offered smiling, knowing that he was the only celebrant for miles.

Hugh was happy to keep everyone busy and Elizabeth was feeling so good herself, having her son back that she was glad to finally have something they could all celebrate. Inviting their two daughters-in-law Jane and Mary, along with Ann, upto her bed chamber she announced

'We have to find you a dress, Ann. I may have something upstairs that you might like.' Elizabeth had some lovely clothes that Hugh had insisted he bought for her to wear at the Burgesses festivities but only one or two she felt were suitable for this particular occasion.

'Try them on Ann,' urged Elizabeth. Ann felt embarrassed. She wasn't used to so much attention *she left all that to John. John had always been comfortable in the limelight. He was born to entertain, and when he put on his puppet shows...* A smile crossed Ann's face at the memory.

Ann finally chose something simple: a cream low-cut blouse with a frilled-squared neckline and blouson sleeves complemented with a grey skirt and corded petticoat to give shape to her fuller figure; topped off with a brown bodice decorated with black edging to bring out the shapeliness of her figure.

Elizabeth had a further surprise for them all. Whilst Ann had been trying on the clothes, she pulled away from the corner, a leather-bound object. It was tall and heavy and Jane had to help her to move it near to the window to allow the sunlight to reach it. Everyone was curious.

'Are you ready Ann?' She asked excitedly, *it was nice to have womenfolk to share things with.* Moving behind the object Elizabeth opened doors and called Ann over to her, a smile of pride and joy on her face as she gestured to stand in front of her for the big reveal… Ann faced the item and was shocked!

'What is it? Is that me?' Taken by surprise Ann recoiled. What was she seeing? She looked about her at the three women. Not sure what to do! Elizabeth laughed.

'It's you Ann. It's called a mirror.' Grabbing her by the shoulders reassuringly, she turned her towards her reflection. 'It's you… you look beautiful!

Ann looked at herself. Excited and a little bit afraid, she looked around at the younger women who rushed to see what all the fuss was about. *She really did look pretty*, admitted Ann, now admiring herself in the mirror. The room became filled with excited screams as the young women each took a turn at seeing themselves in the mirror. Elizabeth walked away and sat down on the bed. It had been such a long time since she'd spent so much time with other women and it was lovely listening to their chatter, but also quite tiring. She smiled with contented pleasure at Ann. Finally, Ann would be getting the marriage she'd always wanted. The wedding that she herself had never had, but she wasn't envious in any way. She was content to be with the man she'd loved all her life, and especially these past few years. If she were to die today, Elizabeth would be happy. Hugh had been a complex man, firm but fair, she knew that, even though he may not show it too often, nor tell her in so many words, he did love her and she would do anything for him.

The bride-to-be looked beautiful, happy, but something was still missing. Elizabeth knew exactly what it was and left the room leaving instructions for the wedding clothes to be removed and set aside for the morrow.

Outside, Hugh could hear the sound of giggling women, a sound he wasn't used to. He could hear his wife talking animatedly as she entertained her female company, she was in her element. It got him to thinking about his own marriage to Elizabeth. They'd just said a few words and signed something in front of a justice of the peace as he was needed back on the island as soon as possible. She'd never complained, never asked any more of him then a thought struck him. He would follow John's lead. He would ask Elizabeth to marry him that very night!

Hugh didn't stop to think. He was used to giving orders and for once, since this whole epidemic started, he felt in control again. The doctor had administered John's *miracle* potion to as many of the residents of the island that he could. All over the island there were reports of people recovering for the disease that had spread wildly through the land and now was a good time celebrate, a double wedding. He was sure John wouldn't mind a double wedding and the reverend... well he was his son, how could he refuse family? His mind made up, it was priorities first – to get Elizabeth alone while she was in a good mood. He needed to be sure she would accept and he didn't want the embarrassment of being refused publicly.

As the day went on, Hugh started to become a little apprehensive. Now that he thought about it he wasn't so sure of Elizabeth's answer. He hadn't been the best husband to her, what if she said no? Hugh tried laughing at his momentary doubts. *He knew his Elizabeth*, he told himself, *she had loved him for years. She was his rock, his comfort, his joy.* When he was in one of his moods, *of which he was aware there had been many over the years,* she knew how to calm him. She listened, and in her silence he saw things through her eyes, she was his conscience, his muse – she'd say yes, he was sure of it!

Chapter Twenty Five

A double wedding

John finally had a few moments to himself to reflect on all that was happening. He'd never felt such happiness since his first few months with Ann. The new, exciting rush of love that had overwhelmed him when he was young, were nothing compared to the feelings he had at that moment. He'd almost lost her...

Something or someone had been looking after him on that journey. Someone maybe had been listening to his prayers? Who or whatever it was, had kept him safe, safe enough to get him home, to save his wife and for that he would be eternally grateful. He'd almost died himself, in his attempt to save her, his gratitude held no bounds!

He looked up to the stars twinkling brightly in the cloud-free sky and his heart... His heart was so full it felt like it would burst with everbounding joy; a joy that filled his whole body. To say he was feeling love just didn't express what he actually felt, it was 'more'... He could find no words to describe it! All he knew was he wanted everyone to share the feeling, even if they could only feel it for a moment. *If this is Heaven,* he thought *then I am not afraid of dying.*

Hugh saw John returning home and decided it was as good a time as any to discuss his idea of a double wedding with him, before he lost his nerve.

John had never seen Hugh so nervous, but when he heard his suggestion, he couldn't be more pleased for him. It was a splendid idea he told him and gave him a hug. What better way to spread his own sense of joy, but to share such a happy time with his friends. The two men shared a moment. Almost instantly, embarrassment hit them both at the same time. They pushed one another away and laughed.

'Ahem, hmm, hmm...' Hugh cleared his throat to speak. 'That's great! Ahem, hmm, hmm' still struggling to clear his throat, 'Well, it looks like we both have work to do.'

'Ermm, aaha... ermm. I guess so.' Mocked John smiling as he too awkwardly backed away from Hugh, his head bowed in embarrassment. 'What have we got to do exactly?' puzzled John.

'Well for one, you'll have to dig out your best suit. The ladies are looking after Ann as we speak, and they certainly sound like they're having fun. I need to think about how I'm going to pop the question to my wife!' he laughed. Well I'll take my leave of you now, John and maybe... (ahem, clearing his throat again) maybe we'll see you at supper this evening, last night and all that..?'

'Maybe' replied John as Hugh walked away.

A gift for Ann

Staring across to the big house for a moment, John's elation was calming down as he walked home slowly. Practical things to consider… He saw Jack tending his horse and had an idea. Give Ann something special to remember her day by, a gift maybe? He wandered over to Jack's waggon and got to chatting about the events of the day. Jack suddenly became excited. He remembered something he'd come across on his travels. He foraged about in the waggon, then handed John a small box.

'It's a wedding ring – made from solid silver.' He told him. 'It was meant to be a salt spoon, part of a set. The silversmith made them 'specially for one of his customers. He was burgled before they could be delivered and this one was all that remained, just look at the engraving on that… the work of a craftsman. He'd engraved it just as the customer had asked too! It seemed a pity to waste all his hard work, so he turned it into this ring, such a delicate design. I'd like you to have it… for your Ann.' He smiled.

'I couldn't possibly.' John refused, shaking his head, handing back the box to Jack, but Jack wouldn't take it.

Ann had never complained about the wooden ring he'd given her when they married, and he wasn't too sure she'd want any other, but then Jack insisted John take the small box. When he opened it he knew Ann would love it!

'If it weren't for you, John, I might never have found my mother – please - take it. I want you to have it.' Jack gave a grateful smile and pushed John's hands away, insisting he kept the gift. John accepted graciously and was about to set off back home when another small box caught his eye. Oval-shaped black ebony with wavy vine-like markings along its side and what looked like leaves engraved along the lines. Its lid was hand-painted with a picture of a man and a woman holding hands, trees were either side of them, and their roots joined beneath the feet of the couple. Above and on both sides of the picture were swirling spirals in a deep red and below were the words

"Your Heart And My Heart Are As One"

'How much?' asked John, determined to repay Jack in some way for his kindness. 'The box would be a gift to Ann the engraved words say all that I feel, *as one at last!*' Jack pretended to haggle with John as he didn't want to offend him any further. He could see John was a proud man. In the end the two men reached an amicable agreement on price, a price that satisfied them both. They said goodnight and parted company, Jack getting back to his horse and John back home. All John had to do now was speak with the reverend and sort out his baptism for the morning.

A son's blessing

Hugh had almost reached the house when he saw John heading towards Jack's waggon. He could still hear the women talking inside and decided that the wisest thing he could do now was stay out of the way of the women-folk. It seemed it could be a good opportunity to speak with Jack, maybe get to know him a little before supper.

As he approached, he realised he didn't know what to say to him. Hugh could normally talk to anybody, but for once in his life, he found himself without words. *What do you say to a twenty four year old son you never knew existed? I guess we're about to find out,* thought Hugh, holding out his hand in greeting.

Jack jumped down from the cart to greet his father and smiled warmly, confidently. Shaking hands, Hugh observed that his son had a good, firm handshake and looked him firmly in the eyes... he liked that, the sign of a man with character. He held his hand and pulled his son towards him proudly patting him on the back before releasing him, then began looking around the waggon with interest.

'So... tell me... how long have you been trading like this?' Hugh had instinctively found the right topic. Fortunately, Jack loved to talk about his work. He talked about his wife and daughter. He talked about his travelling. He talked and talked... Hugh smiled as he listened. It wasn't long before they were talking like old friends, as if they'd known one another all their lives - it felt good.

Daylight was fading and Jack was still finding things to talk about, it may have been nerves making him so chatty, but Hugh was glad of it - it felt natural somehow, it also gave Hugh the confidence to ask him the question that had been on his mind all afternoon. There was a moment of silence as Jack took a breath…

'Jack?' he began, 'There's something I've been meaning to ask you…' he paused, summoning up all the confidence he could.

'And what's that?' asked Jack.

'It's about your mother.' That got Jack's attention as he waited to hear what Hugh had to say. 'Well, she and I, well we were apart for a long time. I didn't even know about you,' he faltered apologetically. 'We only met up again four years ago, after I became a widower.' Jack listened silently. 'We realised we still loved each other right away. I had to get back to the island, to my sons, and I didn't want to leave your mother behind, not again, not this time. We were married by the local justice of the peace. Like Ann, your mother never had the wedding she deserved… well, the thing is…' Hugh struggled, feeling awkward 'Will you marry me?'

'What?' Jack started laughing.

'No, no… that's right.' Hugh was embarrassed. He was making a fool of himself. He'd said it now, it was out there, he may as well get it over with… 'What I mean is… I would like to ask you for your mother's hand in marriage, a double wedding - tomorrow. That's assuming of course that she'll have me.'

Jack stood face to face, toe to toe with father, looked him straight in the eyes and turned away as if in deep contemplation. Turning, walking back, a serious look on his face as if considering his next words with care. No words were necessary. Jack threw his hands in the air and walked straight towards Hugh smiling widely.

'Of course!' he almost shouted excitedly. Hugh shushed him, looking back at the house. He had yet to ask Elizabeth. Jack hugged and patted his father on the back unexpectedly and once Jack had finished seeing to the horse and secured the waggon, he grabbed the items he'd gone to fetch for his wife, they headed back to the house in contented silence, smiling conspiratorially all the way.

'So where've you two been?' called Elizabeth as the two men walked through the door. 'What have you two been up to? You both look like the cats who've got the cream' she scolded mockingly, glancing at the women inside. 'Dinner's almost ready, where's John and his son, we're all hungry here?' Elizabeth was in a playful mood after a great afternoon with the other women and seeing his wife in such a good mood made Hugh feel a little more confident about popping his question, he just had to pick the right moment.

Everyone was beginning to take a seat at the table just as there was a knock at the door. Alice, the housemaid answered it, and smiled as she saw John and his son standing at the door with a large wooden box.

'Jo-o-h-h-n?' called out Ann with a bemused, low, drawn out call of his name, she knew what was coming and laughed as she saw her husband carrying in his one and only life-long possession, an old trunk that had once contained everything he owned, all his possessions, from England. These days it contains his puppets. After their son was born he had started to carve them. They represented his adoptive family back in England and he wanted his son to know all about them. Each puppet held a special memory, a memory that John shared with his son, in the form of a puppet show, just like he watched his mother perform when he was young. Over the years, John, like his mother, had started entertaining all the children living on the plantation, and then the island; they all loved them; especially the part where John made the puppet of himself sing and dance.

'It's for after supper' he announced to the room, struggling with its bulk to find somewhere to put it down. Finally, he and Junior set it down behind the sofa and joined the others at the table. Alice closed the door behind them and rushed to the kitchen excitedly to tell everyone about the treat that was to come.

Dinner was filled with excited chatter, both families coming together for the first time. There was so much to talk about, and whenever there was a moment of silence Jack would fill it with one of his anecdotes about his travels. As with any dinner party people often break into two's and three's and by the end of the meal, just as conversations were running out for the evening Hugh called for silence –

'Now come on, John show us what treat you have in store for us.' coaxed Hugh, taking charge of events for the first time that day.

'Yes, John, come on… show us what's in the box' cried the other guests.

'All right, all right… Now, when we had dinner parties back in England, we would all do what mother called our party pieces. We all had to sing or dance or recite poems for our supper.' He smiled looking 'round at the guests. 'Each one of us here must do something to entertain the rest of us and I'll finish, or should I say we'll finish the night, yes that's you Ann and Junior you know the story as well as I do' he laughed. 'Who's going to go first?' John looked round at each one of them with an encouraging smile, daring each one to go first.

'Come on, let me out of my seat, I'll start it off,' announced Jack confidently, taking a small pipe from inside his jacket pocket. He exaggerated coughing and spluttering to clear his throat, whilst waving his elbows and licking his lips before placing the pipe to his lips. He was actually, quite good. Jack played a jolly jig to that got the feet tapping. Everyone applauded as he took his bows and he grinned from ear to ear, as he mischievously looked from one then the other at his father and mother, stopping at his mother…

'Mother… you're up?' he looked questioningly at her over the table and grinned. 'You always used to sing beautifully at your aunts' Christmas gatherings… come on.' he teased her. Elizabeth shook her head in mock embarrassment, allowing herself to be *cajoled* into standing up to sing.

Hugh hadn't realised what a beautiful voice his wife had. He couldn't even recall ever hearing her sing for that matter. He began to realise just how much he'd taken her for granted over their few short years together and he felt ashamed of himself. Work had taken priority over everything else after his first wife died. He loved Elizabeth, he'd known that for sure, but watching her with her family, seeing her smiling, happy face, hearing her sing… it was like seeing her for the first time. A woman, beautiful, vibrant and… why had he allowed such a gap to grow between them? Just how much had they missed out on? He watched her as she sang and applauded loudly when she finished. Standing up as she retook her seat. He took her hand and… he was about to make his announcement and ask his question, but suddenly –

'Who should go next mother, it's your choice?' called Jack. Hugh sat down as his wife looked around the table…

'I think John's son, Junior should be next.' Elizabeth announced, wanting to involve their guests.

'Come on Junior, get up,' called John; Ann joined in the cajoling of their son.

'No, no. It's been a long day, I'm tired' he replied 'Jenkin is tired, too – look!' Everyone looked over to where the child sat, his arms raised excitedly in the air as if volunteering his turn. He was nowhere near ready to sleep. Others joined in, urging him to take his turn. Reluctantly, Junior allowed himself to be persuaded. Grabbing his wife's hand, he pulled her to her feet and asked Jack to play one of his jigs. Throwing Jenkin onto his shoulders, the child grabbing his father under the chin, he and his wife danced a jig the best they could. Everyone cheered as they clapped to the speed of the dance and applauded them well as they sat back down, exhausted.

'Who's next, who's next?' called Elizabeth, thoroughly enjoying the entertainments. Pointing to each person at the table, she stopped at her husband 'Hugh… come on Hugh, it's your turn.' Elizabeth teased. 'I insist.

As head of this household, and this family...' She looked round the table as everyone sat waiting. 'You - have to lead by example.' She announced boldly.

'Hugh... Hugh... Hugh...' everyone called and started clapping 'til he stood up. Pushing his chair back, in a pretence of being dragged to his feet reluctantly, he stood up cleared his throat, loudly.

'Ahem,' taking in a deep breath, turning towards his wife, he began - 'Shall I compare thee to a summer's day? Thou art more lovely and more temperate. Rough winds do shake the darling buds of May, and summer's lease hath all too short a date. Sometimes too hot the eye of heaven shines, and often is his gold complexion dimmed; and every fair from fair sometime declines, by chance or nature's changing course untrimmed. But thy eternal summer shall not fade, nor lose possession of that fair thou ow'st, nor shall Death brag thou wand'rest in his shade, when in eternal lines to time thou grow'st. So long as men can breathe or eyes can see, So long lives this, and this gives life to thee.' Looking a pleased with himself Hugh bowed and kissed his wife's hand as he finished his recitation and smiled.

'Well done my love, come... sit back down.' Elizabeth proudly praised Hugh. 'Now who will be next?' She smiled round the table.

'I think we have enough here for a small cotillion don't you think? Suggested John. 'So that's Jack on his fife, I can play the fiddle, and you my dear Ann, would you consider playing your drum tambourine for us pretty please?' John gave her his cheeky smile, *how could she ever say no to that smile*, she thought returning his glance with her own bemused smile.

'But I see no fiddle or drum!' Hugh remarked, trying to wriggle out of it, *a man of his age shouldn't be dancing those sorts of dances, they're for the kids, too much jigging*, he grumbled.

'Never fear, John is here!' called John with a wink and skip to his wooden trunk like a child. 'Have music will travel' he grinned, retrieving said instruments from within his box. 'Now come on boys and girls, ladies and gentlemen… to your feet.'

Taking the now sleeping toddler from Mary's arms and laying him on the nearest sofa, Junior and Mary took the floor, followed by Richard, who gladly grabbed Alice, to be his partner, Hugh and Elizabeth that left Jane sitting on her own cradling her baby.

'May I have the pleasure?' asked Reverend John offering to take the baby while she stood up. Placing baby Lilibet carefully on the opposite side of the sofa to Jenkin, he took her hand.

'Are we all in our places? Do we all know what we're doing?' John called to the couples excitedly preparing to dance, men pushing furniture aside, women straightening their attire. There was nodding and shaking of heads, so John walked them through the dance once, giving instructions as clearly as he could in the hope that they'd remember something of the dance at least. Whatever was about to happen, John was sure it would be fun.

'OK then... Each couple stands facing one another a few feet apart, and the next couple stands next to them, and so forth. Now all together, in time to the music, men and women walk forward and back three times. The first couple at the bottom then casts off in opposite directions to skip on outside of rows meeting at the other end grabbing each other with both hands and skipping down the middle do this three times. Are you all getting this?' Everyone shouted yes, 'Still holding hands, the first couple dances under the arch made by the second couple's hands, yes that's right Richard, then over the third couple's hands up and under the fourth couple. No Hugh, that's over the third couple's hands... yes that's right...

Now, holding hands all the time until everyone has danced from the bottom to the top of the row do this up to three times.' This was hard work, but John continued describing the rest of the dance while Jack picked up a rhythm.

The trial run was all over the place, everyone was bumping into one another, laughing, then the music signalled the beginning of the dance proper; John started first to play, Jack and Ann followed after hearing a few notes. It was utter chaos, but it was fun, it was all the evening was about.

Everyone was exhausted by the end of the dance, exhausted but happy. As they returned to their seats, Elizabeth noticed how Richard was still holding Alice's hand and laughing. She told her to fetch them all some drinks then join them at the table and to tell all the other staff to come through and watch the puppet show that was about to start. *Everyone deserves to be happy tonight,* she thought as she looked out over her family, all gathered together for the first, and possibly the last time, *for who knows when they would see each other again?* A moment of sadness crept in at that thought, but not for long, the show was about to start!

Chapter Twenty Six

The party was going really well. All guests were getting along nicely and Elizabeth was in her element acting as host. It had been quite some time since she'd enjoyed herself quite so much. Her only concern was how quiet Hugh had been most of the night something was bothering him she was sure.

Everyone was settling down noisily to watch John's famous puppet show. The servants were excited to be joining the family, even young Jenkin woke up in time to see the show.

John, Ann and Junior took their places behind the sofa where the box had been placed and prepared the puppets in the order they were going to appear. There was no set story to John's shows but his Ann and Junior knew how to follow his lead and adlib depending on the reactions of the audience, there was always at least one person heckling Mr Punch, and they were prepared with witty comebacks every time.

Let the show begin

John introduced the show –

'Good evening ladies and gentlemen, boys and girls, mothers and fathers. Before we start the show for you tonight, I'd like to tell you what the show means to me... My mother used to perform her own version of this show when I was just a little boy. Yes, I was little once.' The audience laughed. 'She told me how each puppet represented a member of her family or a friend and she loved her puppets. She even put me in her show to make me feel part of her family when I joined them.' He took a bow and smiled. 'I was an orphan you see, and funnily enough, master William Shakespeare, who wrote the sonnet that master Hugh so beautifully recited,' he bowed his head to Hugh, 'William took me in when I was a boy, and gave me a home. I'd run away from the workhouse and he found me hiding behind a bale of hay dripping wet and starving. He was with a girl and making himself *rather comfortable* in her arms I might add' John winked mischievously 'As sorry as he was to have to do it, he sent the girl home and took me to his lodgings. Nothing grand, but it was a roof over my head and food and clothing to keep me warm. He made sure I had food and shelter and all he asked in exchange was for me to work for him, run errands, help advertise his plays at the theatre, whatever he needed me to do, a bit like working here really.' They all laughed as he looked over at Hugh.

Then one day, he was told he had to marry this woman who was having his child but he wouldn't be able to keep me. He introduced me to a lovely couple and their son, travelling players from Italy. They were good to me, we travelled all over. They took me in as one of their own, and gave me a home, my first taste of family life. Their son Nicholas became my closest friend and his parents allowed me to call them mother and father. It broke mother's heart when I told her I wanted to come here, to the colonies. But I had a dream. A dream of a better life filled with adventure. As hard as it was for me to leave, if I hadn't taken that journey I would never have met my lovely wife Ann or any of the people here. You're my family and friends, just as much as the ones I left back in England. I'd like to share my memories of fun that my mother taught me about our crazy madcap family, an irresponsible egotistical father, an overprotective mother and a range of sufferable and insufferable friends. Let us begin... John looked down at his family low down behind the sofa, their makeshift stage and turned his back on his audience momentarily, before showman-like turning round to face them –

John's puppet show

'Greetings!' he called out 'and good evening ladies and gentlemen, boys and girls, are you ready to have some fun?'

'Ye-e-s-s-!' called back the audience quietly, not quite sure what they should be doing.

'I can't hear you' cried John 'Are you ready boys and girls, mums and dads, to have so much fun?' John raised his hands, instructing them to shout louder.

'Ye-e-e-e-s-s!' shouted the audience once again, a little louder this time.
'I can barely hear you. Come on, once again – are you ready?'

'YE-E-E-E-S-S-S!' came the resounding reply.

'Get on with it,' called Hugh playfully.

'Okay, okay, you don't have to shout.' John laughed pretending to wave down the noise with his hands. He took a step back towards the sofa to look behind it for something then turned back to the audience.

'It looks like Mr Punch is fast asleep. Will you help me wake him up?' Everyone nodded. 'When I count to three we all need to shout as loud as we can WAKE UP MR PUNCH, three times! Will you do that for me?' All nodded once again. 'One... Two...' John paused, 'Now you will shout as loud as you can, won't you everyone?' John stopped mid-count teasing his audience for a reaction.

'When's the fun going to start?' called Jack heckling John. John feigned mock anger as he turned round to face the audience, then once again, his hands going up and down he counted with his fingers... 'One... Two... Three! WAKE UP MR PUNCH... WAKE UP MR PUNCH... WAKE UP MR PUNCH.' No sound came from behind the sofa except the sound of loud snoring. 'I think I'll have to go and give him a shake. I won't be a-moment. If you see Mr Punch in the meantime, shout and tell me won't you - promise?'

'Ye-e-s-s-!' John pretended to be walking downstairs as he went behind the sofa until he was out of sight, then in a mock sweet voice 'Wake u-u-p Mr Punch.' Nothing 'Wake U-U-P Mr Punch,' a little louder. Then at the top of his voice- 'WAKE U-U-U-U-P-P-P!!!' and the sound of bangs and knocking of a bed head could be heard. There was a moment of silence then a long very loud yawn could be heard.

'Is someone there?' The distorted voice of Mr Punch could be heard as John placed a swazzle in his mouth to give a strange sound to the voice. No one answered.

Jack called out 'Wake up Mr Punch.' He was starting to get the hang of this heckling lark, *it was quite fun.*

'Who called me? Was it the dulcet tones of my dear wife Joanie?' Mr Punch asked with a sweet, flirtatious voice. Heavy footsteps could be heard on stairs as Mr Punch walks up the same steps that John walked down a moment earlier. Mr Punch appears. He sees the audience and peers out at them. Moving up and down the sofa, he stares at each of them in turn. Alice giggled as he looked at her. 'You're a pretty one' said Mr Punch looking along the row for another female... 'And you... And you... and – oh not you!' He looked at Jack when making his last comment. 'But where's my lovely Joanie? Jo-an - nie... Joanie, Joanie, Jo-a-n-i-e' he called louder.

'I'm he-e-r-e!' replied Joanie, suddenly appearing from the opposite side to Mr Punch.

'Oh Mr P-u-u-n-ch, where a-r-e y-o-u?' She called out sweetly as she searched for him.

'I'm he-e-r-e-.' he called back equally sweetly, also searching for his wife. They kept missing each other, then Mr Punch turned and saw Joanie, he sneaked up behind her and frightened her –

'BOO!' he taps her on the shoulder and makes her jump

'Oh-h-h-h-h Mr Punch, you scared me. Why did you call me? What do you want?'

'Give 's a kiss.' The audience giggled a little with embarrassment at the word.
'Oh, Mr Punch... it's far too early for a kiss.'
'Go on... give 's a kiss...'

'I don't know, Mr Punch' said Joanie shyly 'do you love me?'

'Of course I do' he shakes his head to the audience.

'Does he love me, boys and girls?'

Jack called back 'No he doesn't Joanie.'
'Oh yes I do' calls Mr Punch to the audience

'Oh-no-you-don't' they all called back.

'I do Joanie. I really... really, REALLY, R-E-A-L-L-Y DO love you, now give 's a kiss' Mr Punch grabed Joanie, and she hit him with her rolling pin. He reeled backwards... and sideways... and all over the place, finally falling on his back.

'Oh dear, oh dear, oh dear' a worried Joanie frantically ran about her husband's body, 'Mr Punch, I'm going to fetch the doctor.' said Joanie as

she went to fetch the doctor. Mr Punch stood up and started laughing.'
Joanie could be heard returning with the doctor. Mr Punch immediately lay
back down, but face down instead of on his back.

'Doctor, doctor, Mr Punch is over there on his back. I think he might be
dead.' The doctor walked over to Mr Punch and walks back to Joanie.
'I thought you said he was on his back?' Upon hearing this, Mr Punch turns
onto his back while the doctor isn't looking. Joanie goes over the check.

'He is on his back,' she tells the doctor firmly. The doctor takes another
look at his patient. Mr Punch has turned onto his front again.

'Joanie, come here a-moment,' called the doctor. Joanie walked over to him
to find Mr Punch on his back again. By now, Mr Punch is confused as to
which way up he's supposed to be, on his back or on his front and he keeps
turning, eventually getting caught by both Joanie and the doctor, in mid-
turn.

'You're being very silly Mr Punch, wasting the doctor's time like this.
You're very, very naughty' berates Joanie. 'Good day doctor, sorry to have
wasted your time.' And the doctor leaves shaking his head in annoyance.

'I love you,' said Mr Punch sweetly once more, snuggling up to Joanie,
hoping to stop her being angry at him. Joanie moved away in annoyance
announcing she's going to the shops, and saying bye, bye to the boys and
girls.

The audience called back to her 'Bye, Bye'.

A banjo-playing minstrel called Joey joins a saddened Mr Punch who is sitting on the 'stage', all alone. He entertained the audience with his singing and dancing for a while until he catches the attention of Mr Punch. Mr Punch decides to join in and they dance and sang together, clapping hands and inviting the audience to join in. Everyone was enjoying themselves, until Joanie returned –

'What's all this then?' she demands, disapprovingly. Mr Punch and Joey look at one another. They look at the audience and start to sing and dance again. The audience once again joined in.

'Stop all this nonsense, Mr Punch! I want you to look after the baby for me. Here you are.' She hands a small baby puppet to Mr Punch.

'NO!' said Mr Punch, 'I want to play with my friends.' He indicated Joey and the audience and starts singing, dancing and clapping once again in defiance.

'But I have to go to the shops to get your favourite sausages for teatime Mr Punch. Now here's the Baby.' She passed him the baby.

'Give 's a kiss.' He teases.

'Oh go on then...' kissy, kissy – kissy, kissy, the audience laughed. 'Now here's baby. You will look after him, won't you Mr Punch? Maybe you could teach him how to walk?' she suggested hopefully. He carried the baby to Joey and pushes him into his arms and walks away.

'No!' shouted his new friend and tosses the baby back to Mr Punch. He catches it but immediately tosses him back to the minstrel. Baby is thrown back to Mr Punch and Joey quickly leaves Mr Punch alone with Baby. Holding Baby awkwardly, he places him as far away from him as possible and leaves him standing on his own as he walks a short distance away.

'Come to Daddy' he called. The baby started to walk and fell face first. Mr Punch picked him up and again, placed him back where he started.

'Come to Daddy.' Baby falls down again and again. Mr Punch began laughing at Baby as he fell and cried just as Joanie returned with the sausages. Annoyed, she swapped the sausages for the baby and took Baby away, scolding Mr Punch.

'You're a very, very, naughty boy, I'm putting Baby to bed!' Her footsteps are heard noisily walking down the stairs. Mr Punch started singing about the lovely sausages he's going to have for tea when a big green monster with enormously large teeth creeps up behind him and tries to snatch the sausages.

'Behind you!' called the audience. Mr Punch looks round and nothing's to be seen.

'A crocodile... it's a crocodile... it's behind you!' they all shout out once again. Mr Punch turned once again, there was nothing to be seen. Mr Punch asked the audience what did they see?

'A crocodile' they called back even louder than before.'

'A what?' cried Mr Punch.

'A crocodile,' they all called out 'The sausages!' The crocodile had returned to steal the sausages. This time Mr Punch sees him. He grabs the end of the sausages and a tug of war begins until the crocodile finally manages to gobble up all the sausages. Mr Punch is angry, he grabs a nearby stick and forces open, the large jaws of the creature, and places the stick between the jaws to hold the mouth open. He then tries to get the sausages back out of the crocodile's tummy, putting his head into the crocodile's mouth. The audience called out to him

'Don't do it!' but Mr Punch ignores them and reaches in further, putting his head all the way down the throat of the creature. The audience went wild. They started shouting

'Get out!' The crocodile tried to break the stick with his jaw. Mr Puncha doesn't understand what all the noise is about and stands up straight, when suddenly the crocodile manages to break the stick and slams his jaw shut just as Mr Punch removed his head from his jaws, being missed by fractions of an inch. The audience had been screaming at Mr Punch who was oblivious to the danger all the time. The crocodile disappears with the sausages, but they're now dangling from his mouth and Mr Punch starts looking for him.

'Here kitty, kitty, kitty,' he calls. The crocodile appeared randomly around the stage then hid just as Mr Punch was about to turn and catch him. They kept missing one another, playing hide and seek, the audience called out to Mr Punch every time, trying to tell him where the crocodile was to be found. The whole room was in an uproar. Mr Punch didn't hear them, he can't see the crocodile. Eventually he gives up looking and tells the audience doesn't believe them.

'It's naughty to tell lies to Mr Punch, boys and girls. Only shout when you see the crocodile.' The crocodile reappears and Joanie sees the creature, his large mouth full of big teeth and she shouts to Mr Punch in a fearful voice

'Oh… Mr Punch, what is that creature?'
'It's a kitty kitty. It purrs like a kitty cat' said Mr Punch

'A kitty cat?' she repeated 'I just don't believe it, I've never seen a kitty cat that looks like that, Mr Punch!'

'Well he's eaten our sausages!' he told her.
'Eaten our sausages, Mr Punch? How could you let him eat our sausages like that? Now what am I going to cook in my frying pan?' Frustrated and angry, she hits Mr Punch over the head with her frying pan' Mr Punch rubbed his head and looked at the audience for sympathy.

John's puppets continued in the same fashion for quite some time. He told the story about the time his father got drunk with his rowdy friend Scaramouche. He told how Mr Punch tricked the Beadle into putting his own head in the stocks and had rotten fruit and vegetables thrown at him. John told the story about when Mr Punch kissed Baby's nanny Pretty Polly and got hit over the head by Joanie out of a fit of jealousy. His show continued one story after the other with his own puppet, Joey, popping in to sing and dance with the audience from time to time and tease Mr Punch. The stories were full of whimsy and satirical comedy. The audiences participation made it all that much more fun, even the heckling was enjoyable, but every good thing has to come to an end and soon Mr Punch and Joanie were saying good bye. John, Ann and Junior were met by applause from everyone. It was time for a final celebratory drink. The party ended.

The guests were tired but happy. But no one wanted to be the first to leave. Hugh had to be the bad guy and tell everyone to leave, it was late and he still had one more thing he had to do.

Finally, everyone was gone. Hugh and Elizabeth were alone for the first time that day. Elizabeth sat near the fire opposite her husband and closed her eyes, smiling. She couldn't remember when she'd laughed so much. Hugh smiled too as he watched the face of his beloved... They sat in companionable silence for a while. Hugh lit his pipe and looked upon her radiant face, flushed with excitement. The firelight revealed the wrinkles around her eyes, but to him, he saw only the young woman he'd fallen in love with. *If only she could smile like that when she looked at him* he thought.

Hugh left the room silently so as not to disturb her. Taking in the air after smoking his pipe helped him relax. The lateness of the hour meant the island was silent except for the occasional sound of animals grazing, the hoot of an owl or insects mating. Hugh loved this time of night. It was the calmness he loved most, listening to nature at its best, the worries of the day falling away. As he finished his pipe, he knocked out the old tobacco and put the pipe aside to cool. Inhaling the coolness of the air, a sense of peace filled his very being. *Today had been a good day to live,* he thought, savouring the moment.

Unexpectedly, he felt a hand on his shoulder. Startled, he turned around sharply, his instinct as a soldier, taking on a defensive action. Elizabeth had woken from her light slumber to find herself alone. Faint light from the fire's embers showed the lateness of the hour and moonlight revealed the silhouette of her husband on the veranda. Hugh's startled features changed to smile as he realised who it was. Elizabeth, carrying a blanket, placed it about his shoulders, huddling herself in her shawl. *It had to be now or never* decided Hugh, taking in a deep breath to help build up his courage.

The proposal

'Elizabeth...' a look of seriousness on Hugh's face. 'I love you.'

'I love you too' she replied, curious as to where this was leading, Hugh was not one to reveal his feelings. For a moment, Elizabeth became anxious, she'd been so wrapped up in the excitement of seeing her son again, and helping Ann with her wedding preparations that she'd totally overlooked how her husband might be feeling after discovering he had another son. She'd feared his reaction for so long that it now threatened her very being. *Would he be disappointed with her... Ashamed... Angry?* All the things she'd been afraid would happen came flooding back.

Hugh took her hands in his, his head bent in thought.

'Elizabeth?' he looked up and the expression she saw on his face confused her. 'You mean all the world to me you're like the silver moon, shining brightly above the seashore; full of passion and desire. You have given me freely, all the love you can give and I have taken it all and still reached out for more. I have been blinded by your love and have not seen until now, that you are all I want and all I need. You're like the brightest jewel in all the sky and you're standing right here, next to me.'

Elizabeth couldn't believe her ears as Hugh continued with such outpouring of emotion.

'Can you ever forgive me..? I fear not, for it would be like asking a snail to run. I am shamed by your love. I know in my life I have made some mistakes. I know I've hurt you and I've made your heart ache; but I promise you that I will change my whole life for you. I know I will never again find a love so true. I have locked you in this cage, alone, in this house. I have thrown away the key to keep you for my own; but that's how much I've loved you Elizabeth.'

Elizabeth tried to speak, but was hushed by Hugh's finger touching her lips.

'Dear Elizabeth, tell me you will always be my friend, tell me you love me and... hold me tight?'

Elizabeth's mind was racing all over the place. Where had all this come from? Why now? Confused but pleasantly surprised, Elizabeth held him close and squeezed him tightly as he asked. Unable to speak, she could only listen.

'Look at that sea, Elizabeth. On the surface all calm but underneath lies unseen undercurrents, that's how I feel when I look at you Elizabeth. Age has not changed that. The tide will turn, things between us will change, let me show you just how much I care. Let us walk down by the seashore… Let us ride the waves together… Let me take you there.' Hugh's passion was being roused, unburdened by decorum or shyness, Elizabeth assumed it was the drink talking.

'I don't want silver, I don't want gold, all I want is you my love *to have and to hold*.' Getting down on one knee Hugh looked up into Elizabeth's face, hope in his eyes as he spoke those four little words - 'Will you marry me?

Chapter Twenty Seven

Ann had chosen to stay in the big house for the night – it was a new tradition she'd heard about, *not seeing the groom the night before the wedding;* something to do with the likelihood that the groom would change his mind if he knew what the bride looked like. She mused on the subject, she thought it mad, but at the same time, she wasn't prepared to take any chances, even though he already knew what she looked like!

What meant most to her would be to finally be at peace with her conscience. Marrying John with the blessing of the church would take away the guilt she felt. She loved John dearly, but for years she has felt guilt for choosing love over her religion. Tomorrow their marriage in the eyes of God, would remove that guilt, her parents could be proud of her once again.

For John... she appreciated how he felt about religion. He'd never been one for going to church. She didn't really understand what had changed his mind now - arranging his baptism and then their marriage on the same day... but she was thankful. *Today was going to be a good day to live,* she thought to herself.

Elizabeth came rushing into her room looking a little nervous, yet excited at the same time.

'What is it?' asked Ann. 'You look flushed, are you all right? Not getting sick are you, I need you?'

'No' said Elizabeth, sitting on the bed, with the biggest smile ever exploding across her face.

'Dear Elizabeth, what is it? You're worrying me.'

'Oh Ann, my dear Ann, I don't know how to tell you. It came completely out of the blue. Hugh took me by surprise.'

'You're all right though aren't you, Elizabeth?' a now anxious Ann asked of her friend, taking her by the hands.

'I'm breathless with excitement. Last night…'

'Yes…'

'Last night…'

'Yes, yes…'

'Last night Hugh proposed!'

Elizabeth just looked at Ann, looking for a reaction of some kind. They'd never been exactly what you'd call 'close', but Ann had been the only female she'd known since she came to the island, they had become friends, the only friend she'd ever really known. All the years she had cared for her Aunt, she'd spent in a great deal of solitude or with her Aunt. Elizabeth didn't know what it was like to feel as happy as she did right now. Her heart was fit to burst!

'Well that is amazing and unexpected.' said Ann, a smile of pleasure for her friend crossing her face; 'When?' Ann asked.

'That's what I came to discuss with you. Hugh wants us to be married *today!* I wasn't sure how you would feel about it though.' a questioning look on Elizabeth's face.

Ann could see how happy her friend was. She had expected her wedding to John to be just the two of them... their 'special' day, and for the briefest of moments, Ann felt aggrieved at having to share their day, but as immediately as the thought popped into her mind, she berated herself for being so selfish. How could she begrudge Elizabeth her happiness when she herself would finally feel a *truly married woman*? The fleeting selfish thought passed as quickly as it had been imagined and as she squeezed Elizabeth's hand she nodded her head at the same time as saying yes! They hugged one another from sheer joy then began the task of finding a suitable dress for Elizabeth to wear.

Jane and Mary weren't long in arriving and were told the news straight away. Much like the previous day, they began their search through Elizabeth's 'meagre' wardrobe. Although what was 'meagre' to Elizabeth was a volume of clothes to the other three women! They laughed when Elizabeth said she hadn't a thing to wear! The search was on...

Elizabeth, being the wife of a member of the House of Burgess, was used to attending grand occasions as her husband's escort. He insisted he had the best his money could afford and Elizabeth loved beautiful clothes. It didn't take long to find her perfect dress. She knew Hugh would be wearing his usual dark blue Colonel's suit, his official attire for an officer, so to her it had to be her favourite:

An Anne Boleyn-style dress made out of dark blue taffeta. The sleeves, large and hanging, almost concealing her hands. The vest and skirt, decorated with 'V' shaped lace trims, one the correct way up, the other in reverse. Around her neck she wore a high-neck hand-stitched lace collar tied at the back with a ribbon. The finishing touch was a bow-shaped brooch that Hugh had commissioned to be made for her shortly after she'd arrived on the island, it was made up of various suitably sized pearls from the local sea area surrounding the island with small red precious gemstones around the edges. The ensemble looked beautiful. The white daisies in her hair enhanced her maturing beauty and her smile... Elizabeth couldn't express how she felt.

It was time for Ann to get dressed. Ann felt equally as beautiful, but noticing her once red hair was now pure white, she opted to have primroses in her hair to give her colour.

'I do believe you ladies are ready' declared Mary, Jane and Alice, nodding and smiling agreement.

'Have you both had enough to eat?' Alice had been plying the women with small amounts of food and drink as they'd been dressing, just enough to stave off the rumbling of an empty stomach. Everyone had been too busy and too anxious to eat a great deal, but Alice fussed in a motherly fashion

'The condemned woman has to eat a hearty breakfast' she joked.

To an outsider Alice would have appeared to be over familiar, but she'd worked for Elizabeth and Hugh for such a long time, they treated her more like family.

In the meantime, Hugh and John had been carrying out their own preparations. Hugh had stayed the night at John's after Elizabeth accepted his proposal and threw him out for the night! Servants had been given instructions to press his suit, polish his boots and sword and to take them to Hugh first thing in the morning. John's daughter-in-law, Mary, made sure everyone had been fed and watered and John's suit was pressed and ironed ready for the ceremony, but first the men took John down to the seashore for his baptism by Reverend John. The water was freezing, but he'd made a promise to Ann and he was going to keep it. His decision to enter the water was made easier once the men threw him into the water.

After reminding everyone of the seriousness of the moment the ritual was completed by Reverend John and it was Junior's duty as his best man to provide his father with a warm blanket and clothing for the walk back to the hut.

A hearty breakfast later John and Hugh began to feel nervous. John wanted to invest his time left in thinking up what he himself wanted to say to Ann. They'd already been married by Hugh, but he wanted this marriage to mean something more. He wandered off to think.

Hugh remembered his first marriage back in England. It was all a bit of a blur now and he couldn't remember any vows, but his marriage to Elizabeth had been at court, nothing special, just a couple of lines to repeat and that was that – done! He wondered what his son had in mind, so he went to look for him. He found Reverend John in his own prayer. He could hear him talking to God, talking to his mother, asking for her blessing on his father's nuptials. He finished abruptly and jumped as he heard movement behind him.

Hugh just looked and smiled. He acknowledged with a nod, that he understood why his son was asking his mother for her blessing. When she and Hugh had married, it had been 'til death do us part'. Her death had caused a rift between Hugh and his son. Emotions were running high. Father and son simply looked at one another, words were not needed and hugged.

Chapter Twenty Eight

Renew their vows

Preparations were going well for the wedding. As the island had no church of its own, Hugh ordered that the largest barn be cleaned out to make room for all the guests. A wooden table was to be placed at one end of the room directly opposite the entrance and the hand-carved crucifix that one of the islanders had made after first arriving on the island, was to be placed on the table to turn it into an altar.

Hugh had vague memories of his first marriage. They priest performed the legal part of the wedding outside the entrance to the church in front of all the guests then everyone moved inside where the marriage was blessed, but things were different on the island.

Everyone would already be inside when the bride arrived. The groom and his best man would stand near the altar waiting. The best mans' job was to protect the groom from any attack from outraged family members who might disapprove of the joining together of the two people, but since no objections were anticipated by anyone other than the brides themselves, Richard had been charged with the position of best man for both men. Jack and Junior had the honour of walking their respective mothers towards their grooms. Everything was planned down to perfection...

Back at the house

Reverend John had been very busy from early morning, having completed his baptism of John, but before either of the couples could receive the sacrament of marriage he had to listen to their confessions. The men he had no quarms about but now he had to hear the confession of the brides.

The women were still upstairs when he arrived. Mary and Jane were busy feeding the children. Alice had taken charge of household duties - preparing clothes, instructing the stable boys in how to prepare the horse and trap, and generally ordering everybody around. *What was it about the women taking control when they get together,* Reverend John wondered.

Alice was rushed off her feet. When she saw the reverend approaching, she hurried to greet him, offering him food and a toddy before the ladies appeared, he refused – unable to consider food at that moment. He had never been so anxious about listening to a confession than he was at that moment - his step-mother, no less!

He had just discovered he had a half-brother, what more secrets might he be about to hear? Steeling himself for what he may or may not hear, he sipped on water that Alice had persuaded him to drink. He prayed silently for detachment from his emotions, then later admonished himself for even momentarily doubting for he need not have worried. *What you saw was what you got with mother... and with Ann – nothing to declare.*

The time soon came for them all to leave.

'Your carriage… awaits' announced the reverend, stretching his arm out towards the door as Alice opened it to reveal a beautifully decorated pony and trap. Servants had been working all morning to add daisies, primroses and bows to the trap. Ann and Elizabeth were thrilled!

An upside down box was placed on the ground to help each bride climb onto the back of the trap. Reverend John helped first Elizabeth then Ann before proceeding to take his place up front next to the driver. It was only be a short distance to the barn, but the journey would give the ladies time to sit in quiet contemplation before facing their maker at the altar.

The ride was bumpy but pleasant. Pools of water from early morning rain, threatened to splash their gowns, but as the clouds parted it looked like the heavens were smiling down on them. A rainbow came into view,

'A sign of good luck' Elizabeth remarked to Ann hopefully, trying to make conversation as they were jiggled along. Suddenly, the trap hit something, bouncing the ladies almost off the trap, mud splattered everywhere! Ann screamed. Elizabeth grabbed hold of the side and automatically pushed her hand across and in front of Ann to help hold her on. The ponies came slowly to a standstill as the driver stopped to check they were all right and the reverend checked on the women. A bit shook up maybe, but they were both well enough to continue.

Finally, reaching their destination, a little worse for wear but unharmed, they were greeted by Jack and Junior and helped them down from their carriage.

'You look beautiful' said Jack taking hold of his mother's hands and looking her up and down, a delightful smile of appreciation on his face.

'Stop it, oh, stop it - I'm a mess!' she exclaimed. Jack ignored her fussing.

'You'll be fine' he said reassuringly, 'what's a bit of mud between friends?' He kissed her on the cheek and hugged her, happy to be giving her away to the man she loved and the father he'd never known he had.

Junior followed suit. Ann was more relaxed about it. She knew that it wouldn't matter to John what she looked like. He loved her and that was all that mattered. The two men raised their elbows for the ladies to hold and walked them to their beloveds.

Reverend John had already wished Ann and his mother good luck before rushing ahead to take his place by the altar, standing proudly in front of his father and friend. They looked distinctly nervous he noted. Richard, as the only best man, stood resolutely and proud beside his father. *There would no need to fight any parent's of the bride's today.* He knew his position was purely for show.

A fife and drum suddenly struck up its music as Jack, Elizabeth, Junior and Ann began walking towards their husbands-to-be again. The celebrant smiled at them reassuringly, nodding to the grooms to take their places directly in front of him. Jack was first to reach the men, and proffered his mother's hand to his father. One slight error, he'd placed her to the right of him.

'Wrong side, wrong side...' whispered his father in mock annoyance. *Nothing was going to spoil this day for them, not today.*

Jack shuffled his mother to the left of his father and apologized, grinning apologies as he did so. Junior was next... he presented his mother to John with a slight laugh at Jack's shenanigans. *If nothing else,* he thought, *it's put a smile on everyone's face.* He'd noticed how anxious Elizabeth was about her dress and how worried Hugh looked, and wondered if Jack had genuinely made a mistake or if he was trying to lighten the mood.

Everyone was finally in position. Reverend John cleared his throat to bring silence to the congregation.

'Elizabeth and Hugh, Ann and John, it is a pleasure to share today's wonderful occasion with you. Many people believe that entering into marriage is the final step in a romantic relationship. A couple meet, get to know one another and fall in love, decide they want to spend their lives together, and then take the final step - marriage.

But marriage is hardly the final step in a couple's relationship; rather it is the beginning of a grand adventure! All of you have shared the joys, blessings, and challenges of married life for many years now. Today you want to reconfirm your vows in the sight of God; to receive His blessing on your marriages. You confirm commitment to working together and ensuring your marriage blossoms for years to come. May this blessing and renewal of the vows you took to become husband and wife remind you that despite the stresses inevitable in every life, your love, respect, trust, and understanding of each other will continue to increase your contentment and heighten your joy in living.

Hugh, will you continue to have Elizabeth as your wife and continue to live in this marriage?'

'I Will' said Hugh looking to his wife

'John, will you continue to have Ann as your wife and continue to live in this marriage?'

'I Will' said John, winking at Ann with his great big smile

'Do you both reaffirm your love to your wives, and will you love, honour, and cherish them in sickness and in health, for richer for poorer, for better or for worse, and forsaking all others, be faithful to your wives as long as each of you shall live?'

'I Do' both responded in unison.

'Elizabeth, will you continue to have Hugh as your husband and continue to live in this marriage?'

'I Will' she looked earnestly at Reverend John, then at Hugh, smiling happily.

'Ann, will you continue to have John as your husband and continue to live in this marriage?'

'I'm not too sure...' she smiled teasingly at John, 'I suppose... if I must - I Will' she couldn't help grinning mischievously at John. Reverend John scowled at her frivolity.

'Now you have to take this serious or we may as well stop right here and now.' The reverend rebuked Ann. I will proceed. Do you Elizabeth... AND Ann' pausing to insist on being taken seriously, 'reaffirm your love for your husbands, and will you love, honour, and cherish them in sickness and in health, for richer for poorer, for better of for worse, and forsaking all others, be faithful to each of them as long as you both shall live?'

'I Do' both women responded in unison.

'I believe you wanted to say something yourselves? Elizabeth... Hugh proceed.'

Personal vows

Hugh had not had time to give his vows any thought, it had all happened so quickly. As he turned towards Elizabeth and took her hands in his, he cleared his throat hoping the right words would come - they didn't. Elizabeth knew Hugh was not a man of words, but he was a man 'OF his words'. Staring into his eyes, she squeezed his hands tenderly

'Hugh, my love... I have loved you all of my life. You gave me our son' she looked over at Jack and smiled 'Through him, you have been my strength, my reason for being my reason to live. Now, standing here before our family and friends, and in the sight of God, we can live together in wedded bliss, our hearts, minds and body truly as one.'

'I too, Elizabeth, vow here and now to show you just how much I love you. I haven't been the best husband to you... up to now, but I swear, here, in the eyes of God, that I will be a better husband... I promise.' He glanced at Reverend John who took a momentary pause before continuing:

'Now to you – Ann... John.' Have you prepared any vows?'

'I need no preparation, your reverence.' John took Ann's hands as he turned to face her.

'Ann we have been together now for...' John paused to try to remember how many years they'd been married but failing '... well, a very long time.' He said. 'I couldn't have asked for a better wife and mother to our son. You have stood by me through thick and through thin. You have nursed me when I've been sick and worked hard by my side, to make a home. You have my love always and forever. I have but little to ask of you -

In the morning when we wake, if the sun does not appear, will you be there?'

Ann replied 'I will be there.'

'In the dark, if we lose sight of love, will we hold each other's hands and have no fear?'

'I will have no fear as long as you are near.' Ann had her own question to add

'If I feel like being quiet, or I need someone to listen?' John replied with a smile-
'I will be here, have no fear' John knew she was referring to his habit of constantly chattering, and added one final question –

'In the morning when we wake, if the future seems unclear..?'

'I will be here, I will be near.' She kissed his hands. Looking at the priest for permission, he nodded that she could speak if she wished

'John, you have been my hero, my saviour in all things.'

'At least twice now' interrupted John, the father scowling at him once again. Ann continued... rolling her eyes before speaking,

'Twice now' she repeated and smiled before continuing

'As long as there is love, I will cherish you. As long as there is life, I will love you. As long as the stars shine above, I will want you. As long as there are waves in the ocean, I will need you. As long as there is heaven above, there will always be our love.'

John put his arms around her, in front of the wedding guests, he didn't care. The moment was pure love and he had to hold his wife.

'If we're quite ready..?' Reverend John interrupted 'I would like to continue.'
Another momentary pause to compose himself
'On your wedding day, you all exchanged rings as a symbol of the never-ending circle of love; rings serve as a reminder of your vows to one another, and your commitment to living in unity, love, and happiness. At this time, I ask you to reconfirm the meaning of the rings you wear.

Please join your left hands together Hugh, John place your hands on top of Elizabeth and Ann's and repeat after me.'

To Hugh: 'Elizabeth, I wear this ring you placed on my hand - as a symbol of my love and commitment to you.'

'Now, with Elizabeth's hand on top, Elizabeth, please repeat after me –

Hugh, I wear this ring you placed on my hand as a symbol of my love and commitment to you.' She repeated gladly.

'Now John, repeat after me - Ann, I wear this ring you placed on my hand - as a symbol of my love and commitment to you.

'and Ann with your hand on top, Ann, please repeat after me -
John, I wear...' John suddenly interrupted Ann and took a small box from his jacket pocket revealing the silver spoon wedding ring he'd been given by his new friend Jack. He opened the box before Ann and showed her its contents.

'I'd like you to wear this ring if you will?' he waited eagerly for Ann to answer. Ann removed it from its box to look at it more closely, it was beautiful, but she returned it to the box –

'John, you gave me my ring when we had nothing but the clothes we stood up in. It was good enough for me then and it's just as good enough for me now.' She looked at the reverend and nodded that he should continue. John closed the box smiling, he handed it back to Jack, blinking and nodding his head in thanks. Returning to his position, he once again took hold of Ann's hands, first with his own hand on top then changing to put her hand on his. The reverend continued –

'Ann, repeat after me - this ring you placed on my hand as a symbol of my love and commitment to you.' Ann repeated, the reverend continued, addressing both couples this time –

'As a renewal of your union to one another, by the joining of hands, the taking of vows, and by the wearing of your rings, it is with pleasure that I conclude the ceremony of renewing the vows of marriage that joined you and binds you as husband and wife. Please celebrate this renewal of vows with a kiss.'

Hugh and John needed no further direction from the priest…

Jack eventually had to signal for the musicians to start playing to get the couples to part and begin their walk through their guests. The air became filled with tossed rice, falling like early snow to the ground. The ponies and trap were waiting outside to take them all back to the house where they greeted their own families and finished their celebrations amongst themselves. Everyone else on the island celebrated the day with food and drink a-plenty. Music and dance could be heard everywhere, as the happiness was shared with all around.

As the only best man, Richard felt it his duty to make his toast the first –

'What can I tell you... Loyal, honest, funny, caring – but enough about me,' joked Richard. 'I'm here to talk about these two happy couples. To John and my father - I have looked up to these two men, all of my life, mainly because they were taller than me as a child.' He looked and smiled at his father. 'The love they have shown me has been my inspiration, and one of the reasons I never intend to have children!' he grinned.

As the laughs and groans subsided, he continued 'But seriously, I'd like you to join me in a toast to these two, young couples... well, quite young anyway, well, young at heart, ermmm maybe not so young at heart...' the more he tried to correct what he said, the more he seemed to be digging himself into a hole.

'Get on with it' called Jack grinning at his half-brother mischievously, and help him to stop digging...

Richard had no idea where he was going with his speech, and his father was giving him a look that said to hurry up too, so he continued 'OK then, raise your glasses please to Father, Mother... John and Ann, I do believe they have each found their perfect matches. To people in love!'

'To people in love,' everyone began clinking glasses. Hugh was next to speak

'Since we're making speeches, I'd like you to refill your glasses ready for one more toast. To my best friend John, and his beautiful bride Ann, I'd like you to join with me in wishing them all the best for their future together. Remember the two things that make a great marriage – having a good sense of humour, I'm sure you'll all agree that Ann has that, and selective hearing' he laughed - 'To John and Ann!'

'To John and Ann'

They all began clinking glasses again;

'Settle down, settle down again, for I am not yet finished. Keep those glasses raised for my exceptionally beautiful wife – you look amazing by the way, Elizabeth... as always. When, like me, you are lucky enough to find the one that makes your heart soar, your one true love, then you should never ever let them go, I have done just that – To my Elizabeth.'

'To Elizabeth,' everyone started to talk at once until John rapped the table for silence.

'Sorry Hugh, I can't let you hog the limelight, not today... after all, having our marriage blessed and renewing our vows, was my idea first, you just copied,' he joked 'I'll keep it short and sweet though so we can all get on with celebrating.

He turned towards Ann as he spoke 'They say you don't marry the person you live with, you marry the person you can't live without, that pretty much sums up my life with Ann. She has been my stalwart and my best friend. And if anyone tries to say my Ann can't take a joke I say – look at who she married. To Ann!'

'To Ann!'

Epilogue

Elizabeth and Hugh's families were finally united as one. Each with their own lives to live, but in the knowledge of a family united through love.

John had found his happiness when he first met Ann; and Ann, always content to be wife and mother with the man she loved, was now the happiest she could ever be; her family now legitimate in Gods eyes, she could never ask for more.

Everyone was looking forward to the future and over the following weeks, the disease that had spread so quickly on the island, ended as quickly as it began. And with it, a revived sense of community spirit evolved.

There was just one thing that had been bothering Ann all day. After what John had done to save her, journeying through hazardous wasteland, almost dying... she would never be able to repay him except...

Ann had to check her facts with Hugh to make sure she understood the legalities correctly, and to see if Hugh was in agreement. Hugh confirmed and agreed to what she was about to do.

For their marriage was no ordinary marriage. It was a renewal of their vows 'in the eyes of the church' it was finally legal.

Hugh as the owner of their indentures had agreed to their marriage. As Justice of the Peace he was able to perform their marriage ceremony, but it had never been registered before.

Upon the ending of Ann's indentures, she received her land and corn as was her due plus - Hugh had given her ownership of her husband's indentures. The way she understood the law, now that their marriage was legalised and registered through the church, which meant that everything she owned was now owned by her husband.

Ann slipped quietly away returning with a piece of paper held tightly in her hands. Signalling to Hugh, he called for everyone's attention.

'Ladies and gentlemen, boys and girls, everyone – pray silence for one last announcement. John - where's John?' The families parted the way to where John was entertaining the children with shadow puppets. 'John!' called Hugh.

'Five more minutes!?' cried John

'No John, come now, playtime is over.' Hugh insisted. John join him next to Ann in front of all their guests and asked for silence once again, Nodding to Ann that she was now free to speak.

'Good evening everyone. I just wanted to say something whilst we're all here together.' Everyone hushed to hear what Ann had to say 'John...' she turned to face him such love and appreciation in her eyes 'Everyone here knows what you did for me, to save my life... almost losing your own life over some shocking two-headed snake-venom' she rolled her eyes as she remembered the site she was shown upon awakening. Everybody laughed 'You old fool!'

'Hey, less of the old there Grandma!' joked John.

'I want to be serious for a moment, John. I couldn't think how I was going to repay you...'

'There's nothing to repay Ann.' Interrupted John

'Be silent a moment John' pleaded Ann reproachfully. John, making light of being scolded by his wife so publicly, stood looking at his audience with a naughty-child look on his face - everybody laughed.

'SILENCE PLEASE!' yelled Hugh, handing the attention back to Ann.

'John... I have here a document that was given to me by your friend... our friend... Hugh.' She nodded apologetically at Hugh.

John suddenly looked serious as Ann unfolded the parchment. 'This...' she showed the opened sheet to John 'is your indentures. Up until today you have been my slave' she grinned mischievously at John and the guests

'A slave to love maybe, for I'm nobody's slave' said John smiling.

'I know John, I know.' She smiled, but be serious for a moment I pray.... For years we have lived as man and wife, we have shared everything. All that I am and all that I owned has been yours except for this one piece of paper, until now.' Ann took the document and tore it in two, handing both pieces to John. You are now a free man!'

Looking momentarily serious, he faced his wife and took the pieces of parchment from her hands. He'd lived a free life with Ann for so long that he had forgotten all about it. He looked over at Hugh questioningly. Hugh nodded. The guests started cheering and parted a pathway revealing the fireplace. To applause of the delighted crowd, John threw his indentures into the fire. A burst of flames flew up the chimney. He turned back to Ann and hugged and spun her round as their friends looked on –

Today was the first day of the rest of their lives!

Indentures of John Punch

This Indenture made the **fourteenth** day of **September 1635** in the tenth yeere of the raigne of our soveraigne Lord King Charles I, etc. between **John Punch** of the one party and **Hugh Gwynn** on the other party. **Witnesseth,** that the said **John Punch** doth hereby promise the said **Hugh Gwynn** to serve him from the day of his first arrival in Virginia for and during the terme of sevene yeeres. there to be imployed in the lawfull and reasonable workes and labors of said **Hugh Gwynn.** In consideration whereof, the said **Hugh Gwynn** doth promise the said **John Punch** to pay for his passage from England to Virginia, and to find him with Meat, Drinke, Apparell and Lodging, with other necessaries during the said terme; and at the end of the said terme, to give him one whole yeares provision of Corne, and fifty acres of Land according to the order of the country. In witness whereof the said **Hugh Gwynn** hath put his hand and seale, the day and yeare above written

From the Author

When I started the story about John, he was just a minor character in my book called 'Joan - put on a happy face'. He'd left England to follow his dream of excitement and adventure in a new world! I later discovered that there was indeed a real John Punch who lived during the same period as my young John.

I began researching him. The first slave of Virginia the headline said. My John would never be a slave to anyone, but it was too good an opportunity to miss!

I had only two historical entries to go on that even proved John Punch existed. Little did I know that my story was about to be born!

Two simple entries but with the second one, unlike any of the other entries on the page, it had a mark drawn at the end of the sentencing, a cross of Jesus. What did this mean? There was obviously something else going on. I searched for further records that might explain the marking, but there was none.

Many of the records held in Virginia at that time had been destroyed by fire in 1676. A fire set by Nathaniel Bacon and his followers. For me, it was fortuitous, for it gave me carte-blanche to write my own version of events which no one could prove to the contrary!

I began to wonder why a married man with a three year old son would desert his family, and why would he go to Maryland where he could be easily found? If he was running away from a cruel master why would he leave his wife and son behind to suffer at his hands? There had to be reason.

I discovered that John Punch was married to a white woman, also an indentured servant. They had a son in 1637. In the absence of a clergyman, the master of indentured servants was allowed to marry them and Hugh Gwynn was a Justice of the Peace he had every right to perform the ceremony, but marriages had nowhere to be registered at that time.

Other considerations were that John was of South African descent and most likely, would be a non-Christian and Ann, it could be assumed was Catholic since Virginia was said to be a haven for Catholics fleeing England from persecution.

It was a mortal sin for a Catholic to lay with a man outside of wedlock in the eyes of the church and since John loved his wife, it made sense that he would want to make this right at the first opportunity he could. So why run to Maryland?

Well a few reasons came to light:

I discovered that in Maryland at the beginning of 1640 the General Assembly ordered that the clergy be required to post marriage banns and 'keep registers of marriages' – Reason one.

Then on 5th July 1640 it was widely known that Father Andrew White would be performing both a baptism and marriage for **Native Indian chief, Chief Kittamaquud** and his people, this was widely publicised across the land well in advance as converted Catholic himself, Governor Leonard Calvert was said to be attending.

Next I discovered that a Father Thomas Copley had purchased along with the Society of Jesus (Jesuit priests), land from Thomas Gerrard for the purpose of founding a mission and plantation in the colony. The mission operated from the manor of St Inigoes which was established in 1637 and by 1639 it is recorded that they were leasing land to labourers who had worked off their indentures. John's indentures were due to end within a couple of years or so. A visit to Father Thomas would take care of two more problems and all he needed was to reach Hugh Gwyn for permission. My story was now taking shape.

John Punch had been accused of being a runaway. Once I noticed the cross at the end of John's sentencing on 9th July 1640 it started to make sense that there was more to the sentence than we knew!

Another relevant piece of information to help understand the curious sentence given to John Punch has to do with Governor Leonard Calvert himself. He and his family had, since 1639, been working on a legal premise called the Act Concerning Religion, later to become the Toleration Act 1649.

As a converted Catholic himself, he was all for supporting the unification of all *Christian* faiths. Christian faiths being the operative word – namely all faiths who believed in the Holy Trinity. Non-Christian based faiths saw a different side of Governor Calvert. His punishments were more severe and for those unlucky enough to have no faith at all, they faced potential punishment by death, those that survived such a strong sentence were considered lucky to be allowed to be alive!

When Hugh Gwynn ordered the arrest of his servants, he requested they be returned to him to received 'condign punishment' at his own hands, but after a further request to the assembly for their return, on 4th June 1640, he was told to write directly to Governor Calvert. That letter cannot be found. This left me with some questions, but was also ideal to use in my story:

-Could it be true that John was looking to be baptized when he 'ran away'?
-Could Hugh have been pleading for mercy for John because he was trying to be baptized?
-Could the sentence John was given, be the only leniency that Governor Calvert could agree upon in order to be seen as a 'fair' man? The fact that John could have been attempting to become a Christian had been the reason his life was saved? I rest my case!

I came across another extract that Hugh Gwynn was told he could not 'dispose' of the three servants, but once again no explanation given.

This was all getting exciting. I hope you enjoy reading my story as much as I enjoyed researching it – Happy reading!

Descendants of John Punch

They say we get out traits from our ancestors and in the case of the descendants of John Punch, I think that could be the case.

John Punch has been the subject of extensive research by genealogists and historians ever since they discovered he was the 11th generation great-grandfather of former United States President Barack Obama. Furthermore, it was discovered that he was the paternal ancestor of Ralph Bunche, the first African American to win the Nobel Peace Prize in 1950. Bunche was awarded the prize for his successful negotiations of a cease fire between the Israelis and Arabs. It is clear that Punch has left a significant legacy, not only through his famous descendants, but also through his impact on history

There does appear to be a pattern within this family of people who achieve "firsts." Barack Obama was the first black president of America. Ralph Bunche was the first African American to receive a Nobel Peace Prize. And John Punch was the first "slave" of the English colonies. This pattern of achievement is significant and interesting don't you think?

Before any of this was even dreamed of by me, I had written John to be someone who loved life, loved adventure and was hardworking and diligent. Those traits were just my imaginings at the time, but to discover these as family traits passed down through the years, was a wondrous discovery! You can even see a family resemblance of these two great men!

Barack Obama
Past President of the United States of America
11th generation great grandson of John Punch
on his mothers' side

Ralph Bunche
1st African-American Nobel Peace Prize
Winner & descendent of John Punch on his
fathers' side

Acknowledgements

One or two people helped with my research on this book and I would like to thank them -

To Tom Edwards for his help in my research about Gwynn's Island and the surrounding waters and environment. His family have lived on the island since the 17th century so who else is better placed to be the Director of the Island's Museum and protector of its history – thank you Tom.

[Website: www.gwynnsislandmuseum.org]

To Christy and Jason Nicholas – Thank you to you both for your time to help a fellow author, for Christy Nicholas is a busy author herself with books available from: www.greendragonartist.com. The Algonquin language is considered an endangered language with less than 2000 people still using it. Algonquin communities are actively trying to preserve their language through community-led education initiatives and university language courses.

And finally, to my long-suffering family who once again gave me their support; each in their own different ways. Alun my muse, who will listen to me time and again going over ideas inspiring me from time to time with his own suggestions. Then there's David who also listens to me going on about my characters… he is probably my strongest critic reminding me often that my characters 'are not really real mother! And Rosie… what can I tell you about her? She is my daughter, she 'hates' reading books, but she has faith in me by telling me she'll watch the television shows when my books are turned into a series – thanks Rosie!

And for all my supporters who follow my posts of social media – I promised I'd get my second book published so here it is – I hope you enjoy it as much as you did @Joan – put on a happy face'

Thank you all of you

About the Author

Carol was born as a baby in the north east of England. She's a about the same age as her hair, but a little bit older than her teeth.

She was widowed six years ago after re-uniting with her first true love just fifteen years earlier. A real life fairytale some have called it and losing her husband was quite a blow, but her family helped her through this sorrowful period in life and with their support, she gradually rebuilt her life.

An entertainment agent by day, Carol threw her energies into her writing starting with her first book 'Joan-put on a happy face' which was published in 2020. Now she's brought you 'Memories Of...' a biographical historical fiction about John Punch, his friends and his family.

We hope you enjoy this fascinating, alternative history for John Punch's life. A man thought to be a slave after being sentenced to life-long indenture when he was only ever a slave to love... one of the first cases of a marriage by indentures? Read on and happy reading!

In Memory of Barry Mottershead 1946-2017

Glossary

Flip - Made from beer and rum mixed with eggs or cream and a few spoonfuls of sweetener such as molasses, cane sugar or dried pumpkin. A poker is placed into the fire until red-hot and then used to whip the drink into a frothy, warm caramelized flavoured treat.

Freedom dues – Indentured servants would sign up for a fixed number of years and dependent upon who they made their agreement with they would be promised a portion of land, seeds or monies or some variations on which to start their new lives.

Jim Crow - All of the myths surrounding Thomas Rice's 'discovery of Jim Crow have one thing in common: They don't explain where it came from, but one story is as follows:

The Reality of the story is that the Character found its roots in the African culture where traditionally, they had folk tales of trickster animals, including birds, such as crows and buzzards who seem foolish, but who always manage to get what they want through cleverness and luck. In the Yoruba culture of West Africa, he is a crow named 'Jim'. The slave trade brought these folk tales to America and 'Jim Crow' was a favourite. Some slaves even adopted a Jim Crow type attitude as a way of coping with their enslavement. They would play dumb or act the fool as a clever way of avoiding work.

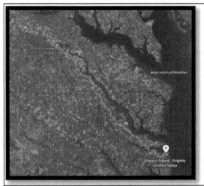

Map of John's journey: Approximately 83miles and thirty hours walk away by today's standards; imagine how much more difficult it would have been crossing the rough, unmarked terrains and wilderness with unknown waters to cross and no tracks to follow in the intended direction.

Image courtesy of Victoria & Albert Museum

Swazzle – This is an item used by Punch and Judy puppeteers to make the characteristic voice of Mr Punch. It is created by using a reed placed at the back of the puppeteer's mouth. Originally swazzles were made from bone or ivory. In performance, the reed is held between the teeth, plugging the mouth except for a small hole through which air is blown, causing the reed to vibrate and create sound. This technique is similar to that used by some North American Indigenous peoples to make flutes. Practice is needed to use the swazzle safely as there is risk of swallowing.

Thornback – A woman is a spinster from the day she is born but over the age of 26 years she becomes known as a thornback

Tidal river - a **river whose ebbs and flows are influenced by tides.** This is usually at the end of a river near the ocean, where water from the sea flows up the river when the tide comes in, raising the water levels. Likewise, at low tide, water flows back out of the river, lowering the water level. The changes in currents can make rivers dangerous to cross.

Topahanocke - was the early colonial name for the town now known today as Tappahannock.

Trenchmore – Cotillion Folk Dance of the times.

Courtesy of playforddances.com

Two-headed Copperhead Snake - rare find in 1654. It would have been scary. Their tails rattle indicating they are venomous and their fang's are still filled with poison and can administer a lethal venom even after death.

Vision quest - A vision quest is a very important Native American tradition and it usually consists of a series of ceremonies led by Elders. It is an attempt to achieve a vision of a future guardian spirit often through the process of fasting, isolation, and meditation. This process is strongly associated with the Native American Indian belief in animism, which is founded upon a belief that all of creation has a soul or spirit.

Inspiration for 'Memories of...'

The sentencing of John Punch – A handwritten copy of the sentencing of John Punch was discovered which began my research into John Punch [courtesy of wikitree]

Indentured servant or slave – It has been disputed for some time whether John Punch was already a slave or an indentured servant. There is sufficient doubt over this to believe that he was an indentured servant or why else would the court waste their time in recording him as such?

Women and marriage – It should be noted that Colonial law on marriage was the same as English law during this period in time and a married woman relinquishes ownership of everything she owns to her husband.

Status of Hugh Gwynn – He was a Virginian plantation owner, a member of the House of Burgess for Charles River County in 1639 and a Justice of the Peace in York County 1941/2.

Registration of Marriages – It was in the early 1640s that the Assembly of Governors instructed the clergy to record banns and register marriages.

Fr Andrew White & Baptism of Chief Kittamaquun - On 05th July 1640 Father Andrew White baptised Chief Kittamaquund, his wife and family, into the Catholic faith following it up with the Holy sacrament of marriage. [Further reading on the subject can be found at mdroots.thinkport.org]

Gwynn's Island 1000 acres of land 1635 – It is recorded that Hugh Gwynn was given land by Pocahontas as a thank you for saving her life when she was young. Although, some historians dispute this story (at the time of writing). He accepted the land in the name of King Charles I. In 1640 he requested a portion of the land be returned to him, to enable him to honour the agreements with his indentured servants that were soon to come to an end. It took a further two years for 1000 acres to be granted and he imported thirty three servants to join him in 1642.

Character Names

During colonial times families often used the same names for sons, fathers, and grandfathers which is confusing to read. The author didn't want to detract from enjoying the story, so in order to simplify the reading, some character names have been changed read on and enjoy 'Memories of...' -

John Punch – Name is real, story fictional – Historically only two facts remain and as a result, he is considered the first slave of Virginia.

Ann Punch – Name and story fictional – Historically her name was unknown at time of writing.

Junior (Jr) – Name and story fictional – Historically the name of John Punch is John Bunch I

Mary Bunch – Name and story fictional – Historically her name was unknown at time of writing

Jenkin – Name and story fictional – Historically his name is John Bunch II

Hugh Gwynn – Name is real, story fictional - Historically known as Colonel Hugh Gwynn, owner of a tobacco plantation in Virginia and with over 1000 acres of land on an island now known as Gwynn's Island

Ann Joyce Gwynn – Name is real, story fictional – Historically known as Ann Joyce nee Burnham, first wife of Hugh Gwynn

Reverend John – Name is real, story fictional - Historically he is recorded as Rev John Gwynn, eldest son of Hugh and Ann

Richard – Name and story fictional – Historically he is recorded as Hugh Gwynn, son of Hugh and Ann

Alice – Name and story fictional, she was the kitchen maid and love interest for Richard [Richard and Alice were named after and in memory of my paternal grandparents]

Elizabeth Gwynn – Name real, story fictional – Historically known as Elizabeth nee Fielding, second wife of Hugh Gwynn. We know this because she was named as his Executrix in 1654/55 which means that Hugh must have died at this point.

Jack Gwyn – Name and story fictional - Historically known as John Gwyn with one 'n' son of Hugh and Elizabeth. There was a further entry covering the same time period for a John Gwyn trader with parents and birth place unknown which led me to the story I told

Jane Gwyn – Name and story fictional – Historically her name is unknown at time of writing this story

Lilibeth – Name and story fictional, I named her after and in memory of Her Majesty Queen Elizabeth II, the pet name given to her by her husband Prince Philip.

Doctor – No name seemed to be needed he is purely a fictional character

Mary-Anne – Name and story fictional, character who started life on the plantation as widow after losing her husband en route to the colony; she began as a scullery maid and worked her way up through the hierarchy of the great house: From scullery maid to kitchen maid to cook and finally to housekeeper.

Septimus – Name and story fictional, character was husband for Mary-Anne who was hired as valet to Hugh Gwynn but died en route to the colony. [Mary-Anne and Septimus were named after and in memory of my maternal grandparents]

Perenelle – Name is real, story fictional – Historically Perenelle was the wife of Nicholas Flamel. It is recorded that 'together' the discovered the elixir for immortality.

Further Reading:

Other books by this author

Joan - put on a happy face

Available in
Paperback ISBN-13: 979-8683476625
Hardcover ISBN-13: 979-8356680090

Author's books are available for reading at
The British National Library - National Library of Scotland
National Library of Wales - Cambridge University Library
Bodleian Libraries of the University of Oxford and
The Library of Trinity College Dublin, the University of Dublin
and many lending libraries in the UK

If you would like to keep in touch with the author you can sign up to her
mailing list at carol.m.mottershead@gmail.com
Don't forget to review the book you've just read
On whichever site you bought your copy

Thank you

CAROL M
MOTTERSHEAD

Printed in Great Britain
by Amazon

28139639R00128